'I'd heard a rumour,' Erica said.

Dr Hurst said briskly, 'I'm not surprised. I made no secret of the fact that I objected to your appointment. Unfortunately I was away at the time, and could only object *in absentia*.' Gregory shrugged. 'The outcome might have been different had I been around. I feel strongly that we've enough chiefs, and not enough Indians.' His smile broadened. 'Even,' he said softly, 'a chief as beautiful as you.'

Dear Reader

NEVER PAST LOVING is Book Two of Margaret O'Neill's quartet, which has more of an administrative setting, and we launch the first of two books by Marion Lennox. A LOVING LEGACY involves general practice in outback Australia; you'll love Richard and Kate's battles. Next month, Richard's sister Christy will be our heroine. FALSE IMPRESSIONS by Laura MacDonald explores occupational nursing, and Margaret Barker returns to Ceres Island again, first met in her OLYMPIC SURGEON several years ago. This time, in SURGEON'S DILEMMA, Nicole's cousin Pippa is the heroine. Happy New Year!

The Editor

Margaret O'Neill started scribbling at four and began nursing at twenty. She contracted TB, and, when recovered, did her British Tuberculosis Association nursing training before general training at the Royal Porstmouth Hospital. She married, had two children, and, with her late husband, she owned and managed several nursing homes. Now retired and living in Sussex, she still has many nursing contacts. Her husband would have been delighted to see her books in print.

Recent titles by the same author:

CHRISTMAS IS FOREVER
HANDFUL OF DREAMS

NEVER PAST LOVING

BY

MARGARET O'NEILL

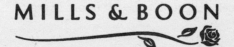

MILLS & BOON LIMITED
ETON HOUSE, 18–24 PARADISE ROAD
RICHMOND, SURREY, TW9 1SR

*First published in Great Britain 1993
by Mills & Boon Limited*

© Margaret O'Neill 1993

*Australian copyright 1993
Philippine copyright 1994
This edition 1994*

ISBN 0 263 78441 X

*Set in 10 on 12 pt Linotron Times
03-9401-53908*

*Typeset in Great Britain by Centracet, Cambridge
Made and printed in Great Britain*

CHAPTER ONE

ERICA turned off from the busy high street of Princes Hollow into the mile-long south drive leading to Princes Park Hospital.

She was quite familiar with the drive, having made three previous visits to the hospital over the last few months, but today, somehow, it looked different. She passed between the lodges on either side of the drive a little way from the entrance, and realised why it looked different—spring had arrived. The grass verges in front of the hedges surrounding the lodges were now, in early March, bright with swaying golden daffodils and pads of primroses. Above the hedges, boughs of trees were smothered with pale, uncurling, tender green leaves.

Her previous visits had all taken place during the winter months, the last at the beginning of February, a wet, grey, dreary day, when the brown, dead bracken and bare trees had been beaded with misty rain. Not that the weather had seemed dreary to her, as she had been on a high with excitement, having landed the plum job of senior co-ordinating officer, following her two previous interviews.

Now, today, on her fourth visit to Princes, she had come not as a visitor, but to stay, as a member of staff. The knowledge was exhilarating, even though the challenge awaiting her was rather daunting. Not, she told herself firmly, that she had any qualms about being able to hold down the job—she had won it fair and square over strong opposition, and knew that she was capable of holding her own. But there was one tiny flaw in the otherwise totally satisfactory state of affairs that had to be faced, and that was the fact that she hadn't as yet met the medical director, Gregory Hurst. He was virtually an unknown factor, and yet he would figure large in her working life, a most important cog in the wheel of life that represented the hospital.

Over her three interviews she had met all the other senior medical, nursing and administrative staff, but Dr Hurst had been away on a lecture tour of Canada and America. That she hadn't met him would not have mattered, she reflected, but she had heard rumoured remarks, during her conversations with various people, that Dr Hurst had been against her appointment. Well, not her appointment personally, but against the creation of the post of senior co-ordinating officer.

The medical director, it seemed, had favoured the employment of additional nursing and technical staff as being more useful than another high-powered executive. Erica, a nurse herself, had some sympathy for his point of view. 'But it'll be up to me to convince him that I'm right for Princes at this moment in time, and that my appointment will help improve the staffing situation eventually,' she muttered fiercely to herself as she drove along.

She rounded the next bend in the drive, lined by rhododendron bushes and tall trees, and unfurling ferns, and met an ambulance coming towards her. Automatically she pulled further over to her side and almost slowed to a stop, though the drive was wide enough to take two vehicles. The ambulance driver gave her a wave as he passed, and that small friendly gesture added to her feeling of well-being and squashed her vague apprehension concerning Dr Hurst.

She smiled and waved back to the driver, and was about to pull away from the grassy bank when a movement on the branch of a tree just ahead caught her eye. Two squirrels were chasing each other up and down the tree. Fascinated by their antics, and with time in hand before her meeting with Matron, she switched off her engine, and sat watching the small creatures.

The scent of pines and wet undergrowth, and cheerful bird song, drifted in through the open windows. Erica breathed in deeply. It was utterly peaceful. She could spare a moment to sit and stare and take in some of her new surroundings. Strange to think that not far away up the drive was a large busy hospital, of which she was now part, full of noise and bustle and the drama of emergencies.

As suddenly as they had appeared, the squirrels disappeared, vanishing into the branches on the other side of the tree. Erica was about to switch on the engine and move on when a flutter of something white above a bush some way into the woods attracted her attention. She stared at it. Was it a large bird, or an early bloom of some sort? No, it was moving too rhythmically to be something blown about by the light breeze, and there was, in any case, hardly any wind in the woods, the leaves hanging still on the trees. The movement looked deliberate. Was someone trying to attract attention? It didn't seem possible, but she could hardly ignore it.

She stepped out of the car and stood on the bank. 'Is anyone there?' she called, feeling rather foolish as her voice echoed loudly in the surrounding quiet. There was no answer. Should she investigate further? It seemed silly; she was probably imagining things.

The white object continued to wave regularly to and fro. The peace and quiet that moments before had seemed so delightful now seemed a little overpowering, the morning air a little too still. Erica, fresh from a large, noisy provincial city, was very conscious of the stillness and lack of traffic, lack of people. She looked up and down the drive. It remained deserted. But, she comforted herself, someone was bound to be along soon, another ambulance perhaps. Meanwhile, she had better investigate, if only to set her mind at rest; it was a situation that she couldn't ignore.

She scrambled down the woodside slope of the bank and made towards her objective through young ferns and scrubby undergrowth. There didn't seem to be a proper path. The waving flag, as she neared it, turned out to be a white scarf, not an innocent piece of paper caught up on a bush.

There definitely was somebody hidden by the bushes, and that someone was trying to attract attention. For the briefest moment she wondered if it could be a trick, and she was being lured into the woods by a prowler. But the moment passed. It couldn't possibly be anything like that on a bright March morning in the peaceful Surrey countryside.

'Hello,' she called. 'Do you need help?'

'Hello,' fluted a wavery female voice. 'I'm here.' The scarf jerked vigorously.

Pushing her way through the last patch of bushes, Erica found herself face to face with an elderly lady lying half propped against a tree.

The old lady looked quite calm. Her faded blue eyes

met Erica's. 'I knew you'd come,' she said. 'I knew someone would come if I waved my scarf.'

Erica thought how nearly she had ignored the signal. She dropped on one knee beside her. 'Hello, love,' she said softly. 'Have you hurt yourself?' One of the woman's legs was stretched out in front of her with the foot everted. Oh, lord, she said to herself, the poor old thing's almost certainly got a fractured femur.

There was no doubt either that the old lady, dressed in a dressing-gown and slippers, had wandered from the hospital — confused, perhaps — though she'd certainly known what to do to attract attention, so she couldn't be too muddled.

'My name's Erica,' she said. 'What's yours?'

'Doreen, Mrs Doreen Howard,' the woman replied promptly. She put out a hand and grasped Erica's. 'And now that you're here you can help me get up, and I'll get back. They'll be wondering where I am.' She winked at Erica. 'They didn't know that I was going to go out, you see; I gave them the slip.'

Erica knew a moment of panic. No way must Mrs Howard be allowed to stand up, as any damage that was done would be aggravated. She didn't seem to be in much pain while she was lying still, but if it was a broken hip, as she suspected, even trying to stand would be terribly painful. She must, without alarming her, make her understand this.

'Mrs Howard, please don't move. You've hurt your leg, and you'll make it worse if you move. I can hear a car coming; I'm going to get help. Promise you won't move.'

Rather reluctantly the old lady agreed. 'Well, as long as you're not too long,' she said. 'I'll wait a bit.'

The way back through the woods was easier than the

way in, because she had made something of a path through the brambles and undergrowth. A Range Rover was coming down from the direction of the hospital. Erica moved out into the middle of the drive and signalled for it to stop.

It halted almost beside her, and the driver stuck his head out of the window to speak to her. 'Trouble?' he asked, one eyebrow raised sardonically as he looked across at her MG parked by the bank. 'Flat tyre? Or have you run out of petrol?'

Erica was furious; he might have a deep, velvety voice, and look incredibly handsome, with black hair going romantically silver at the temples and in wings above his ears, but he was obviously a complete chauvinist.

She ground her teeth, and said angrily, 'It's not my car. There's an old lady in the wood; she's —'

He was out of the car before she'd finished speaking, and striding across to the woods. He was a giant of a man, well over six foot, broad and solid-looking, but he moved fast. Erica had to run to keep up with him. 'Where?' he asked over his shoulder. 'Through here?' He pointed to where she had flattened the undergrowth as she'd pushed her way through.

'Yes,' she said breathlessly. She tugged at his sleeve. 'Look, you go and get help from the hospital. I'm sure the old lady's a patient there. Ask them to send an ambulance and a doctor. I'm a nurse; I'll stay with her.'

'And I'm a doctor,' said the handsome giant. He took her arm. 'I'll have a look at her first and decide about the ambulance.' He squeezed her arm and gave a grim half-smile. 'It's not by any chance Mrs Howard, is it?'

They were almost there. 'Yes, how did you know?'

'Because Mrs Howard is the sort of free spirit who likes to go walkabout from time to time. She's a wonderful old dear, a gutsy lady.' Amazingly, his face and voice softened as he spoke. He seemed a different man from the chauvinistic type who had patronised her moments before.

They reached the patient, and the doctor knelt down beside her, smiled, and took her parchment-thin hand in his strong tanned one.

'Hello, Mrs Howard, what have you been up to this time? Trying to give us a fright again?'

Mrs Howard gave him a tremulous but brave little smile, as if determined not to give in to the pain that she must be experiencing. 'Well, it's a nice day, and I just thought a little walk. . .' She put her head on one side and looked cheekily at him. 'Was she mad, Sister Bee, when she found I was gone?'

'To be honest, I don't know; I don't think that you've been missed yet,' he replied, taking her pulse as he talked, and then moving strong square but gentle hands down her injured leg. He looked across at Erica, who was crouching down at Mrs Howard's other side. 'A fractured femur I think, don't you?' he suggested, all signs of chauvinism gone, seeming genuinely interested in her opinion.

'It certainly looks like it.'

The doctor looked at Mrs Howard and gave her a reassuring smile. 'Well, it looks as if you've broken your leg this time, dear lady, not just a few bruises as before.'

'Dear lady,' scoffed Mrs Howard, looking at Erica. 'He could charm the birds off a tree, that one.' She patted the doctor's hand. 'But he's a good boy.'

'Boy', thought Erica, is the last thing I'd call this handsome, elegant, mature man. She was surprised that he seemed not to mind the old lady's teasing, but he obviously didn't. He smiled down at her gently as he stood up, and then transferred his gaze, without the smile, to Erica.

'I'm going to arrange for an ambulance to get here at once, on my car phone,' he said. 'Please stay with Mrs Howard until I get back, and don't let her move that leg.'

'Of course I won't,' replied Erica sharply. 'I understand the importance of keeping it still until it can be immobilised. I am, after all, a nurse, Doctor.'

He gave a sardonic grin. 'But not one of Princes', I imagine.' He didn't seem to expect an answer; he just looked at her hard.

Erica, to her annoyance, found herself blushing under his dark-eyed stare. Were his eyes a deep, fathomless brown, or black? she wondered. She made herself look straight at him. She still couldn't decide about his eyes, but in the brief exchange she took in the pronounced widow's peak of hair, and the strongly marked black eyebrows, arching over deep-set eyes, large aquiline nose and firm chin. Here was a face of strength and character and dominance, she thought; here was a man who was sure of himself and his place in the medical fraternity. But who was he? Not someone she'd met at her interviews; she would, without doubt, have remembered him. Someone senior — he had to be by his bearing — yet someone who knew and was known intimately by Mrs Howard, a long-stay patient. Who on earth fitted that category?

Her thoughts had taken only a few seconds to flit through her mind. The doctor spoke again. He said briskly, 'I'll be off; just do what has to be done. I'll only be a few minutes.' He bent over Mrs Howard. 'Nurse here is going to look after you,' he said. 'Do as she tells you; I won't be long.'

He turned and pushed his way through the bushes and brambles, apparently unaware of the thorns tearing at his tweed jacket. His shoulders looked massive as he elbowed his way back to his car to make his phone call.

Within a short while he was back, and minutes after his return the woods seemed to be full of people. There was the ambulance crew, and a young casualty officer, and several members of staff going on or off duty, who had stopped to see what the ambulance was doing parked on the drive. The whole area, empty such a short while before, was suddenly busy with vehicles and personnel.

Erica stayed with Mrs Howard until the ambulance team arrived, and then backed silently away. Everyone knew the elderly lady and her talent for going walk-about, and teased her gently while showing concern. Although the ambulance team took over when they arrived, the doctor, who obviously had a rapport with the patient, remained with her and supervised proceedings, and then escorted her to the waiting ambulance. Everyone present seemed only too willing to do his bidding, and she guessed that he must be one of the many distinguished consultants on the staff.

Slowly she made her way back to her car in the wake of the little convoy, together with the other onlookers. Several people smiled and nodded to her but didn't speak. Most of them seemed to know each other, but of course didn't recognise her, and must have assumed that she was a visitor. She was very conscious of being on her own, and not as yet an accepted member of

Princes' staff, but was comforted by the thought that she soon would be.

The doctor seemed to have forgotten her existence. She shrugged, and tried not to mind. After all, she had done what she could for the patient, and that was what mattered, and the doctor, however patronising towards her when they had first met, was obviously super at his job. It wasn't surprising that she had slipped his mind, with all that had happened.

As she reached her car, the ambulance pulled away, and the doctor, after looking at his wristwatch, strode briskly across to his Range Rover. He was clearly in a hurry, and Erica, seated in her MG and hoping that he would at least wave goodbye, watched him as with smooth, swift movements he settled himself into the driver's seat, fastened his seatbelt, and started cruising down the drive.

Disappointed that he hadn't noticed her, she watched in her driving mirror as the Range Rover began to gather speed and move away. It was almost at the first bend when suddenly it stopped, the rear lights went on, and it began to reverse fast back up the drive towards her.

It took a moment to register that he was coming back to speak to her by which time his chunky vehicle had come to a halt beside her MG.

He leaned out of the window and stretched out a hand. His dark eyes met hers. He looked very large, very assured and very handsome. After a moment's hesitation, Erica put her hand in his. It seemed to be lost in his strong, capable one.

'I must apologise,' he said in his deep voice, 'for nearly disappearing before thanking you for your help. If you hadn't found dear old Mrs Howard. . .' he shrugged '. . .it could have taken hours to discover where she was, and she would certainly have been in a far worse shape. Many thanks.'

'I'm glad that I was around.'

He smiled. 'And so am I, Ms. . .'

'Lang, Erica Lang.'

'Miss Lang, of course.' He continued to smile, but it seemed to Erica that the tone of his voice changed, was suddenly remote, flat, and his dark eyes darker. 'I might have guessed. You're taking up your appointment today. We should have met before; I'm Gregory Hurst, medical director.'

Erica stared into the dark, brooding eyes of the man opposite. She became aware that her hand was still in his, and withdrew it slowly. Her mind raced. Here was the man whom she had both wanted and dreaded to meet. The man who, so rumour had it, wasn't in favour of her being at Princes. She should, of course, have guessed who he was; the ambulance crew and the casualty officer had been so deferential. And she had been aware from the first moment they had met of his authority and arrogance, attributes of seniority which obviously came as second nature to him.

His commanding air when dealing with the recent episode was only to be expected, but his gentle manner with old Mrs Howard, which softened his arrogance, was surprising. He obviously knew her well, which was unexpected for someone in his exalted position. He really couldn't have much time for hands-on medicine with all his administrative responsibilities, and it marked him out as someone special that he should be so interested in an elderly patient at grass-roots level.

Perhaps he was not such an ogre after all and she

could win him round to her way of thinking. She would
certainly do her damnedest.

All these thoughts flashed through her mind, and she
gave him one of her loveliest smiles. 'It's a pleasure to
meet you,' she said, 'in spite of the circumstances. I
was sorry to miss you on my previous visits.'

Dr Hurst raised one eyebrow slightly. 'I too,' he said
drily. He gave a lop-sided smile as he scanned her face
with an appreciative eye. 'Though perhaps not for the
same reasons as you. You may or may not have heard
that I'm not in favour of this newly created post of
senior co-ordinator-cum-troubleshooter.' He looked at
her even more quizzically, questioning, his eyebrows
arched almost to his hairline.

Erica nodded. 'I'd heard a rumour,' she said.

He continued to direct his piercing gaze at her, and
said briskly, 'I'm not surprised. I made no secret of the
fact that I objected to your appointment. Unfortunately I was away at the time, and could only object *in
absentia.*' He shrugged. 'The outcome might have been
different had I been around. I feel strongly that we've
enough chiefs, and not enough Indians.' His smile
broadened. 'Even,' he said softly, 'a chief as beautiful
as you.'

'That's a very sexist remark,' replied Erica in a tight
voice, feeling a rush of angry colour go to her face. She
was used to compliments and could usually accept them
graciously, but this one riled her. It seemed patronising, full of innuendo, as if perhaps the doctor was
suggesting that her beauty had got her the job and not
her ability, and the committee had been bowled over
by this, whereas if he had been there they would not
have been. Her emerald-green eyes sparkled with fury.
She would have liked to make some smart reply, but

for the moment couldn't think of anything clever or witty to say.

'But true,' said the doctor, his dark eyes appreciative as they examined the near-perfect oval of her face, taking in the high cheekbones, neat, straight nose, the well defined mouth, wide, but not too wide, and long bob of mahogany-brown hair.

'I don't think that's funny,' Erica said stiffly.

'It's not meant to be; as I said, it's the truth.' He looked at his watch, and said firmly, 'Well, enough chatting. I must go; I've a plane to catch. I'll see you in a couple of days or so, Ms Lang. Goodbye.' He released the brake, let in the clutch, and started to move off slowly away down the drive. To her surprise, he called as he moved off, 'Good luck on your first day.' He was perhaps a good loser. Somehow she doubted it, at least not in this context. He would remain a tough adversary.

As before, Erica watched him gather speed, only this time he didn't reverse, but disappeared round a bend in the drive.

She sat at the wheel of her MG and fumed. What a patronising, egotistical male chauvinist he is, she thought, banging her hands in helpless fury on the steering-wheel, and how incredibly infuriating that we should have to work together at top level. She would be hard put to it to be civil to the man. Why, oh, why couldn't he be as pleasant as the surgical director, or Matron, two people who wanted her at Princes and believed that she would do a valuable job? They couldn't have been more welcoming at her interviews, and both had expressed the hope that they might be friends as well as colleagues. Both were level-headed VIPs in the hospital hierarchy and had said how much

they were looking forward to her arrival. But Dr
Gregory Hurst, damn him, the most senior of the three
and next in seniority to the chairman of the board,
didn't want her. He considered her a waste of space
and money.

She tried to quell her anger and come to terms with
the situation. She must come to terms with it, she who
was usually calm and sure of herself and not used to
giving way to temper. It was in fact part of her job to
be cool and collected.

Slowly she took a few long, deep breaths, and began
to feel calmer. She must concentrate on Dr Hurst's
good points — his gentleness with Mrs Howard, which
must surely extend to other patients, unless she was
someone special to him on a personal front, which
didn't seem likely. And the affectionate respect with
which the ambulance crew and the staff seemed to
regard him. The respect had been obvious, but on
reflection she realised that it wasn't awed, and he
hadn't thrown his weight about unnecessarily, just
enough to get the job done. He was obviously well
liked, a good point in his favour.

Erica sighed; the doctor was in a strong position.
Clearly he had the loyalty of his staff, and was kind to
his patients. And yet he had shown this chauvinistic,
hard side of his nature to her. He hadn't pulled any
punches. He hadn't wanted her at Princes, and had
said so. Well, she wouldn't pull any punches either. If
he wanted confrontation over issues that were important, then he should have it, but where and when it was
possible she would use a softly, softly approach. No
sense in antagonising the elegant and distinguished
Gregory Hurst needlessly.

Erroneously he'd intimated that she had used her

beauty and femininity to secure her appointment. She hadn't, but let him beware. Let him worry about other issues that might crop up; she would use every weapon to achieve what she wanted.

She switched on the MG's engine and started up the drive towards the Old House, the heart of Princes Park, where she was to take up residence as one of the senior staff. Neither Gregory Hurst nor any other adversary was going to stop her making her mark on this, one of the most important of hospitals in Britain, with a world-wide reputation for excellence.

Erica Lang, she told herself firmly, you're here to stay, and no male chauvinist autocrat is going to drive you away.

CHAPTER TWO

ON THE morning following her arrival at Princes Park Erica woke early and lay in bed, mulling over the events of the previous day.

It had been a busy and exciting one. There had been the unexpected meeting with the formidable Dr Hurst. A picture of him sprang immediately into her mind like a photograph, emphasising the black and silver hair, with the pronounced widow's peak above the strong, aristrocratic nose. She could see plainly the firm, rather stern masculine features, the resolute mouth and fathomless deep brown brooding eyes as he stared at her across the recumbent form of Mrs Howard. They had been so close for a moment that she had even been aware of his tangy aftershave.

Mentally she shrugged off her vision of the doctor, and recalled her luncheon with the charming matron, Clare Dunn. That elegant, grey-haired lady had been a mine of information regarding everything and everyone at Princes, and had promised Erica that she would give her all the help she could to get started with her job.

'Come to my office at eight-thirty tomorrow morning,' she'd suggested. 'And if you think it will help, we'll discuss a programme of work and get you fixed up with a secretary. I can let you have a list of the committee meetings that are on the agenda over the next week or so, and give you a bit of background on them. Setting up a brand-new department is going to be difficult, especially as your terms of reference are so

broad: listening to people's complaints and ideas as a
sort of agony aunt, and putting them to the board,
sounding out people in all departments, including the
patients, to find out what their views are about the big
issues at Princes. We want everyone locally to be
involved. Princes is their hospital. Nobody should feel
shut out of decision-making. You've got a tough job to
do, Erica, but I'm positive that you're going to do it
brilliantly.'

She went on to say, 'You will, of course, have some
opposition. But don't be put off by that. Fight your
corner. Most people will respect you for that. Our
medical director, for instance, Gregory Hurst, is a very
forceful man and likes his own way where anything to
do with the hospital is concerned.' She raised her
eyebrows, and gave a smile. 'It'll be up to you to win
him round, Erica. He is, beneath his sophisticated
veneer, a kind and splendid person, and a super doctor,
who still manages to find time for grass-roots medicine
in spite of his administrative work. Unfortunately you
won't see him for a day or so; he's in Scotland, on
family business.' Her face softened. 'I'm very fond of
Gregory,' she said. 'He is special.'

Erica said thoughtfully, 'Yes, I formed that
impression,' and explained how she had met the doctor
on her way to the hospital that morning, and how he
had made no bones about telling her that he didn't
approve of her appointment.

Clare Dunn laughed quietly. 'That sounds like our
Gregory,' she said. 'He doesn't pull his punches, but
he will fight in the open, and he's a fair-minded man.
Convince him in an argument, and you will have his
whole-hearted support. It won't be easy, but, for what

it's worth, my unstinting help is yours for any worthwhile cause you put forward.'

It was great to be offered such support. By the end of luncheon she felt that Matron—or Clare, as she insisted that Erica should call her—and herself had formed a rapport, which was important as they would be working closely together. It was especially comforting to receive her offer of help, knowing how Gregory Hurst regarded her appointment. In spite of Clare's comments about him being fair-minded, Erica couldn't help wondering what she might expect from him. Was he interested in the input of the rank and file where decision-making was concerned, or did he consider this the preserve of a handful of people at the top? Was that what he had meant when he had spoken of there being too many chiefs, and not enough Indians? Did he not fancy any more competition?

What a blessing that Matron and others on the board would be firmly behind her in the newly created job.

'I'm one of Gregory's great admirers, and extremely fond of him,' Clare said as they finished lunch. 'But he is strong-minded, and assumes that he has the monopoly on what's right for Princes.' She had leaned across the table, her dark blue eyes twinkling. 'And you know, my dear, he has not. For all his wit and wisdom, he is sometimes wrong, and needs to be reminded of the fact.'

They had taken their lunch in the pleasant surroundings of the refectory, in the Old House, the Queen Anne manor house at the very heart of Princes Park. The refectory could be used by anybody, but in fact it was generally senior personnel and visiting VIPs who made use of its quiet, solid, club-like atmosphere, rather than junior staff, who preferred the modern canteen in the main complex of the hospital.

After lunch Clare took Erica to meet Dora Hubbard, the resident housekeeper in the Old House. Dora lived in rooms concealed behind one of the many doors that opened off the reception hall. The hall, Erica thought, was rather a stately room, but, strangely enough, also homely, welcoming. There was a high moulded ceiling, from which hung a pair of glittering chandeliers, and comfortable leather or cretonne-covered sofas and armchairs dotted around. The floor and panelled walls and the broad staircase rising from halfway down the hall, and branching to left and right to the first and second floors, were of gleaming, golden, well polished oak. The modest casement windows at either end of the long hall were curtained with faded cretonne curtains to match the furniture. A crackling log fire blazed in the monumental stone fireplace in one wall near the massive front door, and there were spring flowers everywhere on low tables and windowsills.

The housekeeper, a round, bouncy little lady of perhaps sixty something, gave her a warm welcome, and assured her that the few pieces of furniture that Erica had sent ahead of her had arrived safely and had been installed in her second-floor flat.

Erica spent a happy afternoon settling in and arranging her personal belongings. She hung her favourite pictures, and moved the small writing-desk to an alcove between the turret windows, windows that gave the flat its name of the Turret Flat. She filled her bookcases, and set up her music system, and small television set, and rearranged the chairs and drop-sided table, on which somebody had set a bowl of yellow crocuses, to her liking. The sitting-room began to look like home.

And so, after a short while, did the pretty, white-panelled bedroom, with her own pale floral curtains at the tiny windows and matching covers on the bed and the little tub chair that she had brought with her.

Now, lying in bed looking round her pretty bedroom, reviewing the events of yesterday, as the early morning spring sunshine spilled through the windows, Erica felt a wave of pleasurable anticipation wash over her as she contemplated her first full day at Princes.

She felt so full of confidence that even the thought of the dangerously handsome and authoritative Dr Hurst and his dislike of her couldn't diminish it. Not, of course, she reminded herself, that she would be likely to meet up with him for a bit, as he was away. For some reason the thought that she wouldn't be seeing the doctor for a while produced a flash of disappointment — odd, considering that he was a powerful enemy, best avoided until she had found her feet.

But the overall feeling of euphoria remained with her as she showered and dressed, and breakfasted on coffee and toast in her minute but well equipped kitchen. She was bubbling over with happiness.

It was still early, much too early for her meeting with Matron, when she made her way down the oak staircase and across the gleaming floor of the main hall to the front door. There were bowls of glowing, multi-coloured hyacinths dotted about the room, filling it with their heavy, delicious scent, and, by the great oak front door, on a low table, a vase of dazzlingly yellow daffodils.

The hall was empty, but she could hear a rumble of voices coming from behind the door leading to the refectory, where people were presumably having breakfast.

Erica let herself out of the Old House into the mild, balmy air of a perfect spring morning. A morning of pale blue skies, and bulbous, fluffy white clouds drifting before a gentle breeze, with brilliant sunshine glittering on the gravel of the large sweep of semi-circular drive that lay in front of the manor house and the nearby administration building.

The admin building, which housed all the clerical and senior staff for the whole hospital, was almost as large as the Old House itself. In former times of unlimited wealth, it had been the stable block, with staff quarters above. Now it provided committee rooms and offices for Matron and senior management personnel.

Erica made her way to the admin building. She had been allocated an office on the first floor, but, before going up, she paused in Reception to study the blown-up aerial picture of Princes Park that took up most of one wall. It was, she decided, the best way to familiar-ise herself with the whole estate and hospital complex, of which to date she had had only a brief tour.

And there it was, all spread out before her, with the Old House and the admin building at the centre of a fan of modern buildings radiating out to the north, the east and the west. There were the reception areas, with a shop and library, and wards, laboratories, X-ray and theatre units, casualty and rehabilitation blocks, all connected by neat glassed-in corridors. To the south lay car parks and drives, splitting off and going in all directions. And dotted about the acres of parkland were little groups and clusters of buildings which were mostly staff residences. At the ends of the north and south drives, almost hidden by trees, stood a pair of red-brick lodges, which also housed senior staff.

It was like a small village, compact, complete, complex, housing a small, intimate community, with all the problems that that implied.

And I, thought Erica, I'm here to help sort out these problems, where they are connected with the work at Princes. It was quite a daunting thought, but a challenge that she relished.

She turned away from the aerial view which she had been absorbing. Well, that's the geographical layout, she said to herself; now for the nitty-gritty — finding out about the people who live and work here.

She ignored the large, old-fashioned lift, and walked up the stairs to her office. To her surprise, the in-tray on her desk, which she had expected to find empty, held several messages. One read, 'Welcome to Princes, may I have a word about hot trolleys?' And it was signed, 'Martin Blake, Kitchen Supplies Manager.'

And another message: 'We need another pair of hands, can you help?' And signed, 'Overworked radiographers.'

A third, rather mysteriously, read, 'Visitors' parking. J. Lennards.'

It took a moment for Erica to recover from the surprise of finding problems already waiting for her attention, and such disparate problems. Could she really help to solve any of them? None of them seemed to be directly nursing-related, the field that she best understood. She squared her shoulders. Of course she could; these people would not have contacted her had they not thought so. As Matron had said, her brief was wide and embraced the whole hospital, and everything was ultimately patient-related. The news of her appointment had been circulated to all departments, and obviously some people, in spite of Dr Hurst's disparaging opinion, thought that she would be useful. The thought was immensely cheering. She wanted to make the medical director metaphorically eat his words, and admit her usefulness.

The rest of the day passed in a busy haze of activity. By lunchtime Erica felt that she had been working in her office for years. Clare Dunn had given her a lot of interesting information at their meeting, and had introduced her to Kate Gentry, who had been appointed her secretary.

Erica and Kate returned to her office and set up the beginnings of a filing system. Kate then made appointments for the people who had been in contact with her — the radiographers, and Martin Blake — kitchen hot trolleys — and J. Lennards, who turned out to be the head porter, Jack — to meet with Erica the following day.

The first entries were made in her desk diary.

At nine the following morning Brenda Thorn, the senior radiographer, called at her office, and she and Erica discussed staff shortages at length. This was a situation that had been under discussion for months, without any result.

'We're just about managing at the moment,' explained Brenda. 'But with the new rehabilitation unit now almost complete and going into action in the next month or so, our workload will start to get heavier. Rehab will want a lot of progress X-rays on patients, and I think that some of the money spent on the new unit should finance extra help for my department; after all, they will need us to function properly. But I can't seem to make the powers that be understand that, hence our SOS to you.'

Erica couldn't promise anything, but after half an hour Brenda departed, knowing that she had at least the support and understanding of the new co-ordinator.

Later that morning she saw Martin Blake, who had been trying unsuccessfully to get finance for new improved hotplate trolleys for transporting food to wards — a lost cause to date, with so many calls on the hospital purse.

After giving the matter some thought, Erica suggested that they might interest the League of Friends in the project; they were good at raising money for all manner of equipment.

'Yes,' agreed Martin rather gloomily. 'But they like glamorous, spectacular things to raise money for, like body scanners, not dull pieces of equipment like kitchen utensils.'

'Well, leave it with me,' said Erica, with more confidence than she felt. 'I'll sound them out; there's no harm in trying.'

The meeting that she should have had with the head porter had to be postponed, as he was off sick, so she still hadn't a clue what 'visitors' parking' was all about. It remained a mystery, and even Kate, her well informed secretary, was unable to help.

Throughout the rest of the day, she was visited by various people who worked in admin coming in to introduce themselves and wish her well in her new job. Towards the end of the afternoon Miles Stockton, the hospital administrator, whom she had met at her interviews, turned up and invited her to dinner that night in the refectory. He was a small, neat man in his fifties, a widower, with iron-grey hair and a military moustache.

To Erica's surprise, he had seemed wholly in favour of her appointment from the start. Now he said, perceptively, as they sat down to dinner, 'You didn't expect me to be enthusiastic about this co-ordinator's post, did you, my dear?'

There was no point in pretending. Erica shook her head. 'No,' she said. 'I thought that you would look upon me as yet another irritation—you know, always badgering you for something that the hospital can't afford.'

'Well, for what it's worth, I'm hoping that you will at least contain the badgering, and help me sort out the wheat from the chaff, by letting me know what is both wanted and needed. I'm all for greater input of ideas. What's best for Princes is, believe it or not,' he said with a wry smile, 'my total concern, whatever you may hear to the contrary.'

Erica found herself warming towards Miles Stockton; he really was a rather nice person, with a dry sense of humour, and a loyalty to Princes that matched Clare Dunn's.

She enjoyed the evening spent with him, and went to bed feeling that she had made another good friend. Yet oddly it was not Miles, or Clare, or any of the people that she had met during the day, of whom she thought as she drifted into sleep, but the rather daunting, enigmatic Gregory Hurst, with his forceful opinions and suave manner. Although it was three days since they had so briefly met, the image of him was strong and exciting, and the idea of doing battle with him over worthwhile causes filled her with a delicious sense of *joie de vivre*. She couldn't wait for him to return to Princes and to meet up with him face to face.

On the following morning, she did just that. She bumped into him, quite literally, on the cinder track that circumnavigated the hospital buildings. She was taking an early morning jog. It was a blue and gold spring morning full of bird-song, with a light mist clinging to the new pale green leaves of the trees, and she was jogging peacefully along when she turned a corner and ran slap bang into him.

They met with a thud, and she would have staggered over on impact with his large, solid form, had he not grasped her arms with both hands.

'Steady,' he growled. He stood her a little way from him, but still kept hold of her upper arms, his fingers feeling warm and hard through her tracksuit. 'Are you all right?' he asked sharply, his high forehead creased in a frown.

'Fine,' she said breathlessly, still winded by the collision. She was very conscious — too conscious — of his hands on her arms, and almost shrugged them off, but didn't. She could hardly do that, since he was only supporting her to keep her steady on her feet, but his hands gave her an odd sensation that made her feel uncomfortable. She stared up at him, suddenly aware of how tall and broad he was at close quarters, and seeing the gleam above his ears where the slanting early morning sun shone on the silver wedges of hair. The silver there, and at his temples, contrasted dramatically with the rest of his vigorous black hair. He really was incredibly handsome, silvering at the temples, and all that nonsense, she thought rather wildly. 'I didn't hear you coming,' she said, for some reason sounding apologetic, though not meaning to.

He grinned. 'Nor I you,' he said. 'Even soft soles make a noise on the cinders, but we must have cancelled each other out as we approached the corner.' He dropped his hands from her arms. 'You're sure that you're all right? You look a bit shaken.'

'Positive, thank you; as you see, I'm still in one piece.' She meant to sound cool and rather aloof, but against her will she found herself smiling warmly up at him.

His smile, which a moment before had illuminated and softened his handsome but stern-looking face, vanished, as if he'd suddenly remembered who she was and what she was doing here, and he didn't approve. He said briskly, 'Good, then I'll be on my way, Miss Lang.'

She stopped smiling. If he could be distant and businesslike, so could she. 'Yes, and I must get on too. Goodbye.'

'Goodbye.' He lifted his hand in salute and started running slowly away from her, but looked over his shoulder to say, 'See you tomorrow; I believe we're both invited for tea at Clare's place.'

'Yes, I believe so.'

Actually, she thought as she jogged on down the cinder path, she believed nothing of the sort. Clare had not said anything to her about Gregory Hurst being invited to tea. She had simply said. 'Do come for tea on Saturday, Erica, and we can have a nice cosy chat. You can tell me how you're settling into your flat and getting the feel of the place after nearly a week, and I can fill you in on the current news.' She had twinkled happily, and gone on to say, 'Princes has as fertile a grapevine as any other hospital, and some of it even reaches the dizzy heights of Matron's office.'

'I'd love to come and chat,' Erica had assured her, realising that the elegant, dignified Clare Dunn, was in a lonely position at the top of the nursing tree, and probably looked forward to an occasional gossip with someone of senior status whose discretion she could trust.

Clare had the reputation, as Erica had already discovered, of being a super matron, loved and respected by most people, and particularly the nursing staff. She was a splendid manager, renowned for her sense of justice and fair play. She and Erica would be working closely together in the future, as their jobs complemented each other, and it would be an added benefit if they could be friends too.

But why had Clare invited Gregory Hurst, of all people, to join them for tea on their first social get-together, knowing how he felt about her appointment to the staff? Was she hoping to influence them work-wise, for the good of Princes, rather than leave time to work it out? She was intensely loyal to the hospital, having served it for more than thirty years; perhaps this was what had inspired her to arrange for Gregory and Erica to meet in the relaxed astmosphere of her cottage, hoping to lay the foundations for friendship instead of animosity. Perhaps she felt that Erica could win over Gregory and overcome his prejudice at her appointment by an early social confrontation. Perhaps, perhaps!

Erica's thoughts squirrelled around as she jogged her way back to her flat. And what about the doctor? she wondered uneasily. What did he think about spending an hour or so in her company? He certainly hadn't

sought her out since his return from Scotland, and after
the first few moments hadn't seemed particularly
pleased to see here when they'd bumped into each
other just now. After that first spontaneous smile, he
had reverted to a stern poker-face. Did he mind Clare
thrusting her on him? Did he feel manipulated? Or had
he perhaps suggested it, seeing an opportunity to win
Erica over to his point of view at future meetings by
exerting his considerable charms. It was a thought to
bear in mind. Obviously he and Clare were great
friends, and he might have persuaded her to invite him
for that purpose. Well, if that was his intention she was
ready for him. No way was she going to allow herself
to be manipulated by the charismatic, chauvinistic
doctor, or anybody else for that matter. She was her
own woman.

CHAPTER THREE

IT WAS pouring with rain and blowing almost a gale when Erica made her way over to the converted gardener's cottage where Clare lived on Saturday afternoon. It was some way from the Old House and the main hospital buildings. The day was a typical March day of high winds; the brilliant blue skies of the morning had given way to great, heaving clouds of grey and torrential rain in the afternoon.

She was sensibly muffled up in a raincoat and waterproof hat for the walk across to the cottage, but beneath the practical external clothes she had dressed with care. Mulling over what to put on, she had admitted to herself that she wanted to look casual but stylish to impress Gregory Hurst, even if it was only for afternoon tea. She refused to analyse her feelings too deeply, but decided that it was something to do with matching up to his air of authority and sophistication, and not letting him better her in any forthcoming confrontation, at least superficially. And to do this she must look her best. He had even managed to look well turned out in his tracksuit when he was jogging, in a casual, informal fashion.

It was all to do with feeling and looking good, she decided, as she plumped for a nearly new tan suede jacket and short matching skirt and an emerald-green cashmere sweater that matched her eyes. She brushed her thick mahogany hair till it shone, put on a touch of make-up, splashed herself lavishly with her favourite

34

perfume, and left her flat to brave the elements and her meeting with the doctor.

Matron's cottage was very picturesque. It was nearly two hundred years old, and stood in a little walled garden about a quarter of a mile from the main hospital block. Even in the rain it looked like something out of a picture book, with its tile-hung walls and porch and lattice windows.

The porch door was opened as Erica made her way down the narrow brick path, and in the doorway stood not Clare, as she had expected, but Gregory Hurst.

'Hello,' he said with a formal but welcoming smile, drawing Erica into a little lobby between the outer and the inner door. 'I'm standing in for our hostess; she got called over to her office on some urgent business. She asked me to apologise and to say that she'll be back as soon as possible.'

Erica blinked the rain out of her eyes and her long eyelashes, and found them meeting his dark, impenetrable ones. She stared up at him in something like dismay, which she made an effort to conceal. It had been bad enough to know that he was to be present at tea with Clare also there, but without her. . .! She suddenly felt terribly vulnerable, as if the presence of this large, handsome man almost filling the lobby was in some way a threat to her, which was ludicrous. She might have to fight him in committee on important but impersonal issues, but here in Clare's cottage, invited like herself for tea, he was just a man. And men, as men, she could deal with. With her beauty, which attracted admiration from males of all ages, she had been managing men since she was a young woman. Gregory Hurst, just by looking down his high-bridged nose at her with those piercing eyes, was not going to intimidate her.

She gave him a brilliant smile, and started to unbutton her raincoat. 'Poor Clare,' she said evenly. 'A matron's lot, I suppose. She's never off duty — the penalty of living over the shop, as it were — Saturday afternoon, or no Saturday afternoon.'

'We all of us who live in or near Princes suffer that penalty, I'm afraid. It's the sort of buck-stops-here syndrome. If you're available you take the knocks.' He placed his hands on the collar of her coat. 'Here,' he said, easing it off her shoulders, 'let me take that. You go through and take a pew by the fire.'

In one deft movement he removed her wet coat and gave it a little shake before hanging it on the old-fashioned hall stand. Erica took off her waterproof hat and tossed her mane of rich brown hair free. 'Will you hang this up for me too, please?' she asked rather haughtily, handing him the hat. The gesture was more to re-establish her self-confidence than anything else, and he nodded and took it from her with the glimmer of a sardonic smile, as if perhaps he understood her reasons for sounding haughty.

She turned from him briskly, and moved into the sitting-room which opened directly off the tiny hall. To her the atmosphere seemed tense, bristling with things unspoken, but his face was bland, inscrutable; she couldn't imagine what he was thinking. He might even have been genuinely glad to see her and not putting on an act because he was deputising for Clare, but, whatever his feelings, his manners were impeccable.

The sitting-room was a long, low, beamed room, furnished with comfortable old-fashioned chairs and sofas, covered in faded chintzes. Erica sat herself down in an armchair beside the blazing fire.

There was a tea tray set out on a low table, with cups and saucers, and plates with tiny sandwiches, cake and biscuits.

'I'll make tea,' said Gregory, following her into the room. 'Clare said to get on with it. Do you want Indian or China?'

'China, please, with lemon.'

'Good, that suits us both.' He went out through another door, which obviously led to the kitchen. He certainly knew his way about the cottage, and was quite at home there. Erica was surprised by his apparent domesticity. Somehow she had thought that he would have resented doing basic chores, but he was whistling happily as he made the tea, as if it was an everyday affair.

I'm the one, thought Erica, who is uptight and nervous, as if on a first date. Pull yourself together, woman, this can't be happening to you. Men, even attractive men, don't usually faze you like this; usually it's the other way about, and they make fools of themselves. Not that that was likely to happen where Gregory Hurst was concerned, however he felt; it would be out of character. He would only reveal his feelings if he wanted to.

He appeared in the kitchen doorway. 'Why don't you put on some music?' he said. 'Clare won't mind, and she has a good selection if you like classics, jazz or forties music; only on record or tape, though, not CD, I'm afraid. That's far too modern for our Clare; she has an affection for her ancient machine.' He pointed to the rather old-fashioned-looking music centre to one side of the fireplace, and a glass cupboard stacked with records and tapes.

'How impressive,' said Erica. 'What a collection. Are you sure that she wouldn't mind? I particularly enjoy jazz, and I'm quite sold on the forties and fifties stuff.'

'But not Mozart or Beethoven, I take it,' he said with an upraised eyebrow.

Was he implying that she wouldn't be capable of appreciating the classics? Surely not, that would be too rude.

She experienced a little spurt of anger, and smothered it. After all, she didn't want to antagonise him needlessly; it was pointless. Yet she itched to say something to wipe that supercilious look off his face. He wasn't going to look so damn disapproving and get away with it.

She said in a clear, well modulated voice, 'Well, I'm not a complete philistine, Dr Hurst. I have my favourites among the classics, but I can't pretend to be a devotee. I feel that I don't know enough about them to appreciate them fully, and the last thing that I would do is pretend.'

Suddenly his face creased into a smile, a seemingly natural smile which even reached his dark, luminous eyes. His intelligent, distinguished face was transformed. 'How refreshing,' he said, 'to find someone ready to admit that. So many people claim to know or understand more than they do about great composers, great writers, artists and so on, just to impress. Personally, I'm almost a complete ignoramus. I'm one of those people who so infuriates the experts by saying that I know what I like, but can't define why. I know a little about it, but not enough, and when I meet really knowledgeable enthusiasts I am most conscious of my limitations.' He stepped back into the kitchen, and emerged a moment later with the teapot. 'Do choose something,' he said, 'for both of us. I'm a Lena Horne and Beatles fan myself. You'll find plenty of the lovely Lena there, but the Beatles, I'm afraid, are rather too avant-garde for Clare. The sixties seemed to have bypassed her for some reason.'

Erica couldn't think of anything to say for the moment. He had surprised her completely with his ingenuous remarks about his taste in music; they seemed out of character. She had expected that he would not only be well informed about the classics, but also only too ready to flaunt his knowledge. But she was quite wrong, unless he was pretending to be more of an ignoramus than he was. Obviously she had totally misjudged him. It seemed that he had a pleasant unpretentious approach to the arts, or was he putting on a clever act for her benefit? Unlikely. No, she must accept that he was a sophisticated man, mature enough not to mind admitting to ignorance in fields other than his own. He had no need to pretend. What a formidable person he was, so composed and sure of himself, but not, she thought, at this moment anyway, condescending.

She became aware that he was looking down at her as she crouched in front of the records, the angle, as she looked up, emphasising his breadth and height. The brown cord tailored jacket he was wearing moulded snugly across his broad shoulders, and the cream polo-necked sweater beneath contrasted with his tanned skin and black and silver hair. Again she was conscious of the air of elegance and distinction that marked him as someone special. Something in the way that he was looking down at her made her hold her breath. It was very quiet in Clare's sitting-room, in spite of the wind and rain beating against the diamond window-panes, which only seemed to emphasise the silence within. His eyes met and held hers, diminishing the space between them.

She made herself move one hand, groped for a record in the jazz section, and held it up without looking at it. 'Will this do?' she asked huskily.

He took it from her, but his piercing near black eyes didn't leave hers. He continued to stare steadily for a moment, then dropped his eyes to read the label. 'Satchmo,' he said in his deep velvet voice. 'That'll do admirably.' He turned away from her and put the record on the machine.

Their eye contact had lasted for only a few fleeting moments, and afterwards Erica couldn't be sure that it had happened at all, or if there had been any significance in it. She might well have imagined it.

Against the background of the husky but melodious voice of Louis Armstrong, they drank their tea, ate a few sandwiches, and talked, after the first few stilted minutes, of everything under the sun.

The terrible famines in several parts of Africa were mentioned, and Gregory revealed that he had been there some years before with one of the medical missions.

'It's almost impossible to imagine, here in England,' he said, his stern face softened by sadness and reminiscence, 'the suffering, and especially the plight of the children. One never quite gets over it. . .their little bloated pot bellies and the rest of their dehydrated skeletal bodies, all for the want of a little water, a handful of dried milk. So little, and yet it's life or death to them.'

'I wonder if it will ever be resolved,' said Erica softly.

'Not for a very long time,' said Gregory. 'What with man-made and natural disasters, there seems no end to their suffering.'

'I wish that I'd gone out there,' whispered Erica, 'and at least tried to do something.'

'Why didn't you?' asked Gregory, his voice brittle, questioning, almost accusing. 'It's hell, but it's worth it; it gives a whole new dimension to medicine. I think that everyone in the medical and nursing profession should go at least once.' He sounded aggressive, angry. 'It gets things in perspective.'

'I was booked to go to the Sudan,' she explained. 'But my mother fell ill—cancer. It was terminal, so I stayed to nurse her. End of story really.' She blinked tears from her emerald-green eyes, and produced a tremulous smile.

Gregory's voice and manner changed at once; he was suddenly gentle, understanding. 'When did your mother die?' he asked softly.

'Nearly six months ago.' She smiled at him. 'It's all right, I'm over it now, and she would be pleased at what I'm doing. She was a nurse.' Her eyes were still brilliant with unshed tears.

'My dear girl,' he said. He had been sitting at the other side of the fireplace, but now he stood up, and moved round the low table to perch on the arm of her chair beside her. 'The death of someone close takes more than six months to get over; it's traumatic, I know. You've been—are being—marvellous. I'm sorry if I was a bit rough just now; foreign-aid work is rather a hobby-horse of mine. We spend hours in committe wrangling about what to spend on this or that sophisti-cated piece of equipment, and at the tiniest fraction of the cost we could save hundreds of lives. And I'm as vehement as anyone, fighting for what I want, but at times I feel guilty about it.'

He put a hand on her shoulder and squeezed it gently. It was very comforting. She smiled up at him. 'You're right, of course, about going to places where help is desperately needed; those who could should. I might try next year even if it's only for, say, a month of my holiday.'

She was glad that Gregory's attention had been diverted away from her personal grief. That she could cope with, without too much sympathy. She was sur-prised that she had said as much as she had to a near stranger. She didn't find it easy to talk about her mother's death. Her heart contracted for a moment; if only she and her mother had not been so close.

Gregory said, 'We're planning a relief trip to eastern Europe in the autumn, before winter sets in. Save some of your holidays for then, and come with us and do some real hands-on nursing.'

Was he being serious? She looked at his face, and saw that he was. He was actually waiting for an answer from her. Well, at least, she thought wryly, in spite of not wanting me here, he is expecting me to stay. That's got to be good.

'Of course I'll come,' she said. 'It's the sort of opportunity that I've been waiting for.'

'Good, I'll keep you to that.'

There was the sound of the front door being opened.

'Ah, our hostess returns,' said Gregory.

He slid off the arm of the chair, as a moment later

Clare entered the sitting-room, arms stretched out in greeting to Erica. 'My dear, I do apologise,' she said, taking Erica's hand in hers. 'I hope that Gregory's been entertaining you in my absence. Such a nuisance being called away like that.'

Erica murmured that it was fine, and yes, Gregory had taken care of her.

'Well, at least it's given you two a chance to get to know each other,' said Clare, glancing brightly from one to the other of them.

For the briefest moment Erica wondered if the emergency had been manufactured, and Clare had deliberately left the two of them together. Well, if she had, it had worked. She and Gregory had got to know each other to some extent, even if they were not, nor likely to be, bosom friends.

'I'll make some fresh tea,' said Gregory, taking the teapot with him into the kitchen. 'What'll you have, Clare?' he called.

'Oh, Indian—strong, please, I need it after half an hour with Lady Violet.' She turned to Erica. 'Lady Violet,' she explained, 'is a rather formidable but influential old lady on our board of governors. She tends to take up causes.'

Gregory put his head round the kitchen door. 'Lady Violet,' he said in disparaging tones, 'is potty. She's always getting bees in her bonnet. What on earth did she want, Clare, badgering you on a Saturday afternoon? I thought your message said an emergency.'

'Can't you guess?'

'Not this nonsense about selling off part of the land for a leisure centre, and letting out the Dower House for alternative medicine or holistic practioners, or whatever they call themselves.'

Clare nodded. 'She's doing a bit of lobbying before Monday's meeting.'

'I don't believe it,' said Gregory, with some fury. 'Well, we'll scotch that nonsense.'

'Oh, I don't think so, Gregory,' said Erica softly, firmly, and almost to her own surprise. 'I've already heard about it — the complementary medicine idea, anyway — from several quarters, and there's quite a lot of sympathy for the idea. We've got to discuss it further. I don't know much about the selling-off of land for a leisure centre — I've only heard of it vaguely — but alternative, complementary or holistic medicine has aroused strong interest.'

Gregory returned with the teapot, filled Clare's cup, and put the pot firmly on a place mat in a hostile silence, and then sat down.

He gave Erica a hard stare, his eyes like stones. 'Don't tell me,' he said in scathing tones, 'that you, a trained nurse, believe in all this rubbish!'

'What rubbish?' asked Erica in a freezing voice, her eyes focused on him angrily.

He shrugged his wide shoulders in a contemptuous gesture. 'Laying-on of hands or spiritual healing, reflexology, hypnotism. . .all that sort of nonsense.'

They stared at each other across the width of the fireplace. The temperature in the room seemed to have dropped. Animosity crackled between them. This couldn't be the same man who only a short while before had spoken so tenderly of the starving children in Africa.

Erica opened her mouth to make a smart retort, and then suddenly remembered where she was, and became aware of Clare's presence.

She swallowed her fury at his contemptuous dismissal

of the whole field of alternative medicine, and managed a smile of sorts.

'Sorry, Clare,' she said, turning to their hostess. 'I didn't mean to start a battle, but clearly Dr Hurst and I don't see eye to eye on this matter. I at least feel that the idea should be aired and not dismissed out of hand, wouldn't you agree?'

Clare smiled at both of them and said, to Erica's surprise, 'I knew that you would be good for each other.' She beamed at Gregory. 'I think you've met your match, dear man, Erica's not going to be the push-over that some of the board and committee members are. She'll fight hard for what she wants.'

'Well, Miss Lang had better take note that I'll fight hard to prevent our resources being used to fund crack-brained schemes that are no good to anybody.' His dark eyes gleamed. 'Schemes that give false hope to people already in dire straits are just not on. I will not see my patients suffer needlessly.'

'But people ought to have the option,' said Erica angrily. 'You shouldn't decide for them; you don't always have to be right. After all, it's not so long ago that psychology was suspect and shell-shocked soldiers were treated as cowards.'

Gregory's mouth thinned into a straight line. 'That's ancient history, Miss Lang,' he said coldly, calmly. 'Psychology and psychiatry have long been scientifically proved to be acceptable.'

'But many doctors were dead against it at one time, putting psychiatry in the same category as you are now putting holistic or complementary medicine — as a sort of fetish believed in by cranks.' She gave him a fiery, challenging look, conscious that she was being very partisan because she resented his attitude. 'How can

you condemn a whole new approach as useless until
you research it more? There are plenty of people ready
to quote actual cases; you just won't listen to them.'

'We can't afford to waste time on what is at best a
palliative, at worst harmful, emotionally if not physically. I've seen this sort of thing in operation at close
quarters,' he said bitterly, 'and have every reason to
distrust it.'

Erica calmed herself with great difficulty; she must
try to convince him that it wasn't always a failure.
'Look,' she said, 'if I can produce say half a dozen
patients willing to explain how they benefited from
alternative medical treatment, will you at least give
them a hearing?'

'Half a dozen are no good as a sample.'

'A taster, then, enough to make you say that it's
worth looking into the various disciplines. Will you
agree to that in, say, two weeks' time and go easy at
the meeting on Monday?'

Gregory looked at her, eyes unfathomable, face set.
He was a stranger, not the polite, pleasant person with
whom she had, such a short time before, shared
'Satchmo' and China tea. 'All right,' he said, after a
few moments' thought, raising a sardonic eyebrow.
'You're on. Within two weeks, six cases documented
and verified. But just the same, if I can persuade
enough people to bypass the whole business, I will.'

'Wouldn't it be fairer to go for a postponement of
discussion for the fortnight you said you'd give me?
After all, if you are so sure that alternative medicine is
totally invalid you have nothing to lose, and I shall
look a fool for going out on a limb and tangling with
you at one of my first meetings.'

'You're willing to risk that so early on in your

promising career?' he asked, in a half-cynical, half-teasing tone, seeming genuinely interested in her reply. His abrasiveness had quite disappeared. A glint of what might have been admiration flickered in his dark, deep-set eyes, which he fastened on hers as he leaned forward in his chair. The silver at his temples gleamed in the glow from the fire. His eyebrows were arched questioningly, and the planes of his face were thrown into relief by the firelight and the soft glimmer from the shaded wall lamps. In Clare's feminine, cosy sitting-room, he looked immensely strong, immensely masculine and unbelievably handsome.

Erica breathed in deeply, trying to ignore the way that her heart was beating an uneven tattoo against her chest wall. She would not be affected by his large presence. No wonder, she thought, he had such a profound influence on hospital affairs; the sense of power emanating from him was remarkable.

Determined not to be overwhelmed by him, she said quietly, 'It's my job to put forward other people's ideas, or defend their right to do so, and I've already heard that there is some interest in alternative medicine, so I must speak out. That's part of my brief.'

'The devil it is,' he said, with a slight grin. He sat back in his chair and made a steeple with his competent fingers. He turned to speak to Clare, who was smiling quietly, apparently unaffected by her visitors' heated exchange. 'You were right, Clare, our new co-ordinator is a formidable opponent.' He stood up in one easy, fluid movement, in spite of his massive frame. He leaned over Erica and offered her his hand, and gave her a wide, generous smile. 'It's a case of "may the best man win", I think, don't you?'

Erica nodded, and put her hand in his, and felt it

grasped by his warm square brown fingers. Notwithstanding his size and strength, the pressure on her hand was gentle and reassuring, and she felt that, whatever their differences, he would be, as Clare had told her, a fierce but fair opponent, professionally.

Their handshake had virtually brought the afternoon to an end. Gregory, pleading pressure of work, had left soon after this, leaving Erica to stay and chat about this and that with Clare.

But their conversation had been general, and, much as she enjoyed gossiping with the matron, Erica longed to get away and mull over her afternoon, and her confrontation with Gregory Hurst.

At last back in her flat, she went over and over the events. There was no doubt that the doctor was prepared, if reluctantly, to be professional, and give her a hearing. That had been confirmed. On the personal front, she wasn't so sure of his attitude towards her. Certainly he wasn't falling over himself to date her, as most men were when they were newly introduced to her and bowled over by her particular brand of beauty. She was sensibly aware that her emerald-green eyes, high cheekbones and flawless complexion, combined with a happy, extrovert disposition proved irrestible to many men. Over the years she had learned how to deal with advances from both old and young men, the sophisticated and the brash, but Gregory Hurst seemed to fall into a different, unique category.

He hadn't seemed to be moved by her extraordinary beauty, even when they had first met on her arrival at Princes, and that in itself was unusual. On their subsequent meeting, on the cinder track, he had been cool, and today, in Clare's cottage, he had been charming, sexy and abrasive, in turn.

He was as much of an enigma as she herself sometimes proved to be to her admirers. She had heard since she had been at Princes that the medical director was a highly eligible bachelor, who, however, somehow kept himself aloof, without giving offence. He was an outgoing personality who joined in, in spite of his rank and seniority, many of the social activities connected with the hospital. He was president of the tennis club, an active member of the drama club, and an enthusiastic squash player. For good measure, he also sang in the chapel choir, and was said to be a superb baritone. In addition to being all of this, he had the reputation of being a workaholic, and dedicated to Princes Park and all that it stood for as a seat of learning and medical excellence.

'The wretched man,' said Erica to the bathroom walls as she lay soaking in a hot tub before going to bed on that Saturday night. 'A paragon of virtue? I reckon he's too good to be true. There's got to be a flaw somewhere.'

CHAPTER FOUR

ERICA spent Sunday morning pottering about her flat while she considered the confrontation she had had with Gregory Hurst the previous day at Clare's cottage. It annoyed her that she couldn't forget him.

She had woken up thinking about him, in a half-dreaming, half-awake state, in which, with good grace, he had completely capitulated to her over her determination to put forward the plans for the alternative medicine project for discussion.

'Fat chance,' she muttered fiercely, as she vigorously polished her little walnut writing-desk. 'I'm going to have a hell of a job convincing that arrogant devil to give way. I hate the wretched man.'

Even as she said it, she knew that this wasn't quite true. She might resent him for his opposition to her and for already exerting his charms over her, but hate him? No. He exasperated and infuriated her by his smooth sophistication, and the calm air of assurance that he carried with him at all times. Yet that same air of elegant self-assurance also attracted her, in a way that his stunning good looks alone didn't. She had known plenty of handsome men of all ages, and many of them had been distinguished, many of them had seemed assured, but their assurance had sometimes been a little superficial, and under stress she had seen them rattled. She had the feeling that Gregory Hurst wouldn't easily be rattled, and that his assurance was rooted in some deep self-knowledge, some inner wisdom.

In her heart too, she knew that Clare had been right about his being fair if he was convinced about something. He wouldn't hold out just to make a point. Well, it would be up to her, as her first challenge, to convince him that it was right for Princes at least to consider the merits of alternative medicine. Perhaps she had been a bit rash to promise six people willing to give evidence of cures or improvement, but somehow, with her secretary's help, she would do so. If necessary they would scour the local practitioners of acupuncture and aromatherapy and other healers, and ask them for case histories, and they would surely get some positive results.

On this resolve, feeling in need of companionship, she decided to go to the refectory for lunch, where she would almost certainly meet someone to chat with. It might even be possible to get the views of a few more people on alternative medicine in the course of ordinary conversation. Any sort of feedback would help in her battle with Gregory Hurst. She was surprised by a prickle of hope, as she descended the wide staircase to the hall, that she might meet up with the doctor himself, but that, she told herself firmly, was not why she had chosen to lunch there. She wasn't even sure that she wanted to see him, and she had no reason to suppose that he would be at the hospital today. She didn't even know if he lived within Princes' boundaries or in one of the nearby towns or villages.

She was about halfway down the stairs when the huge oaken front door opened, and a gust of March wind blew into the reception hall, fluttering the flowers in their vases. There was laughter, and a babble of voices. Even before they entered the hall, Erica recognised Gregory's voice. There was no mistaking his deep velvet tones. Her heart jerked with surprise, and a tremor of pleasure ran through her, which she immediately tried to squash.

A moment later he appeared, his hand beneath the elbow of a gorgeous-looking Indian lady in a brilliant sari partly covered by a multi-coloured cape. A soft, gauzy veil floated gracefully round her head and shoulders. Her brilliant, colourful clothes looked exotic in the polished, homely elegance of the hall of an English manor house. But in spite of them, the Indian woman seemed very much at ease, very graceful. She was laughing up at Gregory, who towered above her protectively, casually immaculate and very British in a fine woollen hound's-tooth checked jacket, and designer cord trousers. The two of them had the appearance of being old friends.

They were followed closely by another couple, an Indian gentleman and a petite redhead, both looking sophisticated and impeccably dressed for Sunday luncheon in country club surroundings. All four were obviously together, and Erica concluded that they must be either Gregory's private guests or VIP visitors whom he was squiring around. This was a distinct possibility as distinguished visitors to Princes Park were often accommodated in the Old House, and, as medical director, Gregory might be involved in their entertainment.

For a moment she stood frozen on the staircase, for some obscure reason not wanting Gregory to see her and feel obliged to introduce her to his companions. Suddenly she was aware of feeling lonely on this, her first Sunday at Princes, with no office to visit, and nothing planned. She looked down on the laughing group below and felt excluded.

Mentally, she shook herself, and put a brake on her imagination. There would be plenty of people she could talk to in the refectory, and this afternoon she would go out in her car and explore the surrounding countryside. Later she would go to the service in the chapel, and perhaps after that visit the hospital social club and renew acquaintance with some of the staff whom she had met during the week. She would fill the day with interesting things to see and do, and not let herself be lonely.

For the first time since leaving her home in Bristol she thought about her large circle of friends there, and especially of Patrick. Patrick, her second cousin, with whom she had virtually grown up, and who thought himself to be in love with her. It was partly due to Patrick, and her own ambiguous response to his declaration of love, that she had decided to move to Princes Park; that and the opportunity to take on a challenging job. Until now, she'd had no regrets about her decision. Bristol, and her work and friends there, was behind her, and she was looking forward to all that her new career had to offer. But now, briefly, seeing Gregory Hurst with his close circle of friends, she felt a twinge of regret arising out of her unlikely attack of homesickness.

'Damn,' she muttered crossly. 'Stop feeling so bloody sorry for yourself.'

Slowly she descended the stairs as Gregory steered his guests into the refectory.

He hadn't even seen her, and when she entered the refectory he was seated at a table on the far side of the long room, with his back to the door.

She had just sat down at a table for two, in the already fairly crowded room, when a short, stocky, fair-haired man who seemed vaguely familiar appeared at her table.

'May I welcome you to Princes, Miss Lang,' he said, holding out his hand. 'I'm Larry Grey. You won't remember, but we met briefly during one of your interview sessions. I'm head of the pain clinic.'

They shook hands, and memory came flooding back. 'Of course, I remember visiting your clinic with some of the other candidates. But I'm sorry, I didn't take much in; it was a very brief visit.'

'Indeed it was. We're rather the Cinderella of the hospital, I'm afraid, the last resort for patients who have unresolved pain that can't be accurately assessed and otherwise treated, the point where conventional medicine seems to fail, so we're not in the front line for visitors.' He waved his hand at the chair opposite her. 'May I share your table?'

'Of course, I shall be glad of your company; and please, let's drop the Miss Lang—it's Erica.'

'Thank you.' He seated himself opposite her, and gave her a nice friendly smile. 'I hope you don't mind,' he said, rather diffidently, 'talking shop on a Sunday, but when I saw you sitting here I just had to grab the opportunity to speak to you. I believe you will be attending the policy and resources committee tomorrow, and that in your capacity of senior co-ordinator you can represent the interests of rank-and-file bods like me.'

Erica laughed. 'I would hardly call you, as head of a clinic, rank and file,' she said, liking his modesty and honesty. 'And I'm sure that you are quite capable of putting forward your own interests. But if I can help of course I shall be only too pleased.'

Lary grinned in response. 'Well, thank you for the compliment, but, as I've told you, the pain clinic is a low priority when it comes to resources.'

'As far as I can make out, everyone wants more money for some project or other,' said Erica, pulling a face. 'I don't know that I've enough clout yet to raise funds for lost causes. But tell me more, you never know.'

'Well, in actual fact the project that I have in mind will bring in funds; it could be a money-spinner.'

'Then I don't see why you need my help, Larry. Surely the committee will jump at the chance to make money.'

Larry pulled a face. 'Not in this instance, I'm afraid; the project is controversial to say the least.'

'Sounds intriguing; do tell more.'

'Alternative medicine,' said Larry laconically, with a lift of his brows.

Erica gave a little gasp of surprise. 'How strange that you should mention that at this moment. I've been thinking about that very subject this morning.'

It was Larry's turn to be surprised. 'Really? How come?'

'Oh,' she said vaguely, 'I was talking to someone about it yesterday, and I understand what you mean by saying it's controversial.'

'Well, I don't know how much you are in the picture, but it seems to me exactly the sort of issue that you should be involved in as an independent authority.'

'Yes, you're quite right; it is within my brief.' She guessed why Larry Grey had pressed to speak to her. She said, 'You've heard about it being on tomorrow's agenda, and about the opposition lobby, and want me to fight your corner. Well, don't worry, I intend to. Of course, I've only just learned about the project, but I'm going to do my best to ensure that it is at least given a fair hearing. I believe the issue has been mooted before, but has never got off the ground.'

'Yes, our formidable Gregory Hurst is firmly against it, and has quite a lobby behind him. I can understand that as a scientist he distrusts any treatment that can't be proved, but, working in the field that I do, one learns to sometimes accept the unlikely, the virtually unprovable, and be grateful for the results. He should occasionally listen to people like me.'

Yes, thought Erica, examining the open, cheerful face of the man opposite her, he should. She wondered if he felt bitter about Gregory Hurst, and the power that he seemed to have. He didn't sound particularly so, just resigned to the invevitable, and yet he was a well qualified doctor of conventional medicine, who surely should be involved in any discussion connected with the issue.

'Tell me,' she said, 'why you believe in alternative medicine, when so many doctors don't?'

'I didn't say that I believed in it blindly, not in all its forms,' he replied. 'But I think that there is something in some of it, and when you deal with the sort of hopeless cases that come my way — cases of intractable pain — any possibility of relief is welcome, whatever the source. My argument is that by giving house room here at Princes to practioners of the various healing arts we could both evaluate their work and exercise some influence. And patients should have a choice, without feeling guilty, when conventional methods fail them and they are out on a limb.'

'You seem to feel so strongly about it, I'm surprised that you haven't tried to do more before to promote interest in it.'

Larry shrugged. 'No time really to get involved. When you have a fight of this sort on your hands against a powerful lobby organised by Gregory Hurst, one tends to take the easy way out. Not very principled, I'm afraid, but fact. That's why having someone like you around will prove invaluable. You have the time; in fact, as I understand it, it's your job to represent factions needing support, even against the mighty powers that be.'

Erica felt a surge of excitement. Here was someone who understood what her role was about, and for a moment she fervently wished that Gregory Hurst could appreciate her as this doctor evidently did. She might be, to use Gregory's words, 'another chief', but she would be a hard-working one. She said softly, 'Well, yes, in principal that's my brief, if I think the cause worth while.'

'And do you think the cause of alternative medicine being given a hearing worth while?'

'Oh, yes, I do, most certainly, and I hope you will help me compile some practical evidence.' She explained about the conditions she had agreed with Gregory Hurst — to produce evidence of six patients helped by alternative treatment.

'Easier said than done,' said Larry, sounding serious. 'You see, it's not so easy to evaluate this sort of treatment by purely scientific standards; one is talking about the whole person, and their reactions.'

'So there's no chance of producing the convincing evidence that I need?' asked Erica, suddenly depressed at the thought that Gregory would win the battle before it had hardly begun.

'I didn't say that exactly; it's convincing somebody like Gregory to accept different criteria of evaluation. After all, some of our foremost teaching hospitals are now participating in such work; I don't see why Princes should drag its heels.'

'If I can persuade the medical director to look at it in that light, will you help me find cases?'

'Yes, I'll let you have a list tomorrow. I know most of the local practioners at least by name or reputation, and I have one lady who has been working voluntarily in the clinic for years, who's had many apparent successes. I've got those catalogued.'

'What field is she in?'

'Laying-on of hands, faith-healing, talking, listening. . . Some people do seem to have a gift, you know, hard as it is to accept. I was as sceptical as the next doctor when she first offered to help in the clinic. But not any more. If all else fails, I ask Betty to help.'

Erica enjoyed Larry's company and his conversation, which was useful and constructive, but all the time that they were lunching she was conscious of Gregory's presence at a table not far away. Once, when Larry was absorbed in choosing a pudding from the menu, she had casually half turned, and to her chagrin had found Gregory looking straight at her. He had inclined his head in a little bow, and their eyes had met, and even at that distance she had been conscious of their dark depths. He had eyes, she thought, that seemed to be able to read one at a distance, and, nodding as coolly as she could in return, she had turned back to speak to her companion.

A little later, as they were coming to the end of their

meal, Larry said softly, leaning across the table, 'Don't look now, but the enemy cometh.'

'The enemy?' she asked, startled.

'Our Gregory, who else?'

'Oh,' she said lamely, and then rallied and smiled. 'The enemy. . .a little harsh, don't you think?'

'Not at all,' said Larry rather grimly. 'He's strong, formidable, implacable. We'll have to fight hard to beat him.'

'Well, we will put the case strongly,' she said, and impulsively put out a hand and patted his, 'for your project to be given a fair hearing.' Dr Grey was a nice man, who deserved what help she was able to give him while remaining neutral over the outcome.

At that moment Gregory arrived at their table. He smiled and nodded a greeting to both of them, as he said caustically, 'Well, Miss Lang, you've wasted no time in discovering a pro-lobby activist for this faith-healing business. Just don't let Larry's enthusiasm influence you too much. Sadly, in his line of work, he has to clutch at straws, but that's all they are — straws.'

'I don't know how you can be so sure of that,' replied Erica sharply, 'as you haven't bothered to find out enough about the subject. And for your information, Dr Hurst, I'm not going to be influenced by Dr Grey, any more than I am going to be influenced by you. I'm the impartial observer, remember; that's *my job*, and I intend doing it to the best of my ability without fear or favour. All I want is to make sure that everyone has their say. Believe it or not, I'm not committed either way.'

Both men looked surprised for a moment by her vehemence. It was Gregory who recovered first.

'Of course, very commendable,' he said smoothly,

and, as far as she could tell, without sarcasm. 'It's no less than I expected of you. Of course you must listen to all sides; I see that.'

'Then why don't you let the committee go ahead and discuss the matter freely tomorrow, as I first wanted, without any pre-conditions?'

For a fleeting moment a triumphant gleam brightened his eyes, but it quickly vanished. 'Ah,' he said. 'Regretting our agreement that we postpone the discussion while you search for reliable subjects to substantiate claims of cures? Are you stuck for candidates?'

'Not at all,' Erica flashed back at him. 'As a matter of fact, we were discussing cases when you left your guests to come over and speak to us.'

It was impossible to tell whether Gregory was affected by this statement, for he simply shrugged his shoulders, and said politely, 'I left my guests to give you an invitation, Erica. I thought that you might like to accompany me on my rounds tomorrow morning. I think that you'll find it interesting. And you'll see what I mean about raising false hopes by promises of magical healing.'

Larry, who all this time had kept quiet, said in a low, angry voice, 'You've no right, Hurst, to make such a remark. You're speaking out of ignorance. I'm no more interested than you in magic, or get-fit-quick methods; you should know that. But when all else fails, hope, with a little help, can work wonders in some cases; not all, but some.'

The two men stared at each other, Larry looking red and angry, while Gregory's feelings were only revealed by a slight flaring of his nostrils.

Erica spoke very softly. 'I think that both you gentlemen are getting carried away with your arguments.' She looked from one to the other of them. 'You're both good doctors and want what's best for your patients, and I'm in between. Why don't you start off on that assumption?' She turned to Gregory. 'I'd like to come with you on your rounds tomorrow,' she said, and he nodded. She looked at Larry. 'And if I may, in the early afternoon, before the policy and resources meeting at four o'clock, I'd like to visit your pain clinic.'

'Please come, any time,' said Larry. 'We're virtually open all hours.'

Gregory gave Erica a wry smile. 'Well done,' he said quietly. 'A nice show of even-handed justice. Long may it continue.' He half bowed to her, and his eyes met hers for a moment. 'I must be off now, before my guests think that I've deserted them. See you at nine tomorrow in my office.'

'I'll look forward to it,' she replied.

Gregory returned to his table, and a little while afterwards left with his party. She stayed and drank coffee with Larry and then excused herself and returned to her room, refusing Larry's offer to accompany her on a tour of the local beauty spots. She felt in her bones that she must hold herself aloof from both Larry and Gregory until she had visited both their departments tomorrow. Any deviation from this would smack of favouring one or the other, and this she was determined to avoid at all costs.

CHAPTER FIVE

ERICA woke on Monday morning immediately alert to the day ahead. Her eyes flew open wide. She was going to do rounds with Gregory Hurst. Infuriatingly, and seemingly beyond her control, her tummy churned with a mixture of pleasure and trepidation at the thought. The wretched man. In spite of his obstinacy and doggedness over the alternative medicine controversy, he drew her like a magnet on a personal level. She had felt it on Saturday even when they were arguing furiously in Clare's cottage. And yesterday, when he had appeared in the hall with the beautiful Indian woman, she had been swamped for a fleeting moment by a wave of pure, unadulterated envy. Envy for the woman, because he, Gregory, was holding her arm.

Envy! The word, the very idea, made her sit bolt upright in bed. She drew her knees up and linked her hands round them. Her heart pounded. It was ridiculous, impossible. You didn't have that sort of reaction about the behaviour of someone whom you hardly knew, even if he was a tall, dark, handsome, super doctor. The adulatory adjectives flowed through her mind without effort. The sheer masculine attractiveness of the man was alarming. Even the mature, unshakeable Matron Dunn had spoken of him as special.

She muttered under her breath, leapt out of bed, and pulled back the curtains to look out over the parkland. The leaf-budding trees and grass were a tender green under the clear, translucent spring sun-shine, the azure-blue skies full of cotton wool clouds sailing before a strong westerly wind. She wasn't sur-prised to hear the weatherman forecasting blustery weather, with fine periods. A typical mad March day ahead.

She too felt slightly mad, slightly disorientated, getting ready to accompany Gregory Hurst on his rounds, her usual sureness about her actions almost deserting her. Normally she would know exactly what to wear for any occasion, but this morning decision-making was difficult. She wanted to be exactly right. For a moment she almost wished that she had a uniform to wear, which would have made the choice for her. She gathered her wayward thoughts and concentrated. Instinct told her to look professional in the presence of the medical director and the patients. Not that he would probably notice what she was wearing, as long as it didn't stick out like a sore thumb. She decided on a black, mid-calf finely pleated wool skirt, a white silk shirt, casually open at the neck, a black and white check jacket, and low-heeled black court shoes.

The result was pleasing. She looked businesslike, she decided, inspecting herself in the mirror after she had showered and dressed, but not too formal to frighten off the patients. She twisted her long mane of mahog-any hair into a smooth, vertical pleat from the nape of her neck over the crown, and secured it firmly. Care-fully she applied cream and powder, a little eye and lip make-up, a light spray of perfume, and was ready for the fray.

The phrase came readily to mind, but in fact she hoped that it would be anything but that. No way did she wanted to get into a battle with or between Gregory

Hurst and Larry Grey. She intended to be a cool, impersonal but sympathetic observer.

This morning, as Gregory escorted her round the hospital, she would listen and learn — learn about the patients, and the man who, as medical director, was ultimately responsible for their care. Of course there were other consultants and registrars directly accountable for their own patients, but, as Gregory himself had said, 'The buck stops here', where Princes Park was concerned.

Half an hour later Erica arrived in Gregory's office in the cardio-thoracic unit. He was an experienced general consultant physician, but she knew that the cardio-thoracic field was his speciality, which accounted for his office being there.

He was seated behind his desk, looking, in spite of the mound of papers in front of him, quite unruffled. He was making a telephone call, and gave her a nod of greeting as she entered.

As usual, he looked distinguished, but at ease, in a charcoal-grey suit with a matching grey tie knotted beneath a crisp white collar. His black hair, with the silver touches at the peak and above his ears, was brushed straight back, looking strong and vigorous. Erica was glad that she had taken trouble in choosing what to wear; it gave her confidence to know that she looked just right in her costume, her feminine but unfussy dress complementing his formal suit.

She stood just inside the door, and returned his greeting with a warm smile. A totally unexpected wave of pleasure washed over her as she looked at him. She squashed it at once and consciously composed her features to look friendly but cool.

He finished his phone call, and put down the

receiver. 'Good morning,' he said, with a smile equally as warm as hers had been. It had a peculiar effect on her, and she felt suddenly breathless. 'Do come in and sit down.' He grimaced. 'I'll not be a moment, just signing a few letters that my dragon of a secretary insists upon, and then we'll be on our way.'

'I'm looking forward to the round,' said Erica, pleased that her voice came out sounding quite normal. Thank God only she was aware of her peculiar response to his presence. She took a chair on the opposite side of the desk.

'Good,' he said briskly. 'I'm looking forward to showing you around, and there couldn't be a better way to see Princes properly than by visiting a wide variety of wards.'

Erica nodded her agreement. 'It's just the sort of tour that I need to really get to grips with the feel of the place. I've visited most of the hospital over the last week, but having a guide like you will make all the difference. Most of the people whom I met were helpful, but I felt rather in the way in some of the busy departments, and guessed that several of the sisters couldn't wait to shoo me out.'

A wide smile creased his face. 'I don't think that you'll have that sort of problem today,' he said, and his dark eyes glinted with humour. 'If necessary, I shall pull rank so that you can see and ask about anything that interests you.'

'Even if it's about something on which you and I don't agree?' she asked, feeling suddenly at ease, her own eyes teasing him.

'Even then, Miss Lang,' he said, his deep voice all at once soft and seductive. 'For this morning, at least, you have *carte blanche* to ask anyone about anything that takes your fancy.'

Their eyes met, both holding laughter. For one mad moment Erica wanted to say that *he* took her fancy, and wondered with a sort of inward hysterical giggle what he would say if she did. She lowered her eyes to conceal her ridiculous thoughts from him, and reminded herself that this was a prosaic working day and flights of fancy just weren't on. But in spite of this salutary reminder, one part of her guessed that he had the sense of humour that would appreciate the joke, and she would have loved to put it to the test.

She brought herself back to earth with a bump by reminding herself that she and Gregory Hurst were sharply divided on at least one issue, and that undoubtedly there would be more situations when they would be on opposite sides. It was too soon in their relationship to test his sense of humour; she must wait and find out about that, as about many other things.

Blinking to remove the sparkle of fun from her eyes, she said in rather a prim voice, 'Well, thank you, Dr Hurst. I'll bear that in mind.'

He looked at her rather sharply, briefly surprised by her change of manner, but his own eyes, which had looked a soft dark brown during their exchange, were now expressionless and almost black as they met hers.

He gave an abrupt nod. 'Right.' His voice was all brisk efficiency. 'I've nearly finished.' He signed several more pieces of paper, his eyes rapidly skimming over the contents of each, and put them in his out-tray. He stood up, towering over her as he leaned forward, his large, well kept hands on the desk. 'Ready, Miss Lang,' he asked pleasantly, 'to come to grips with life at the grass roots?'

Erica stood up, but, in spite of her slender height, felt dwarfed by him. Her eyes were still several inches below his. She tilted her head back, and was able to look him straight in the eye.

'I'm ready,' she said, determined not to be overwhelmed by his large physical presence and even larger personality, 'for anything.'

Gregory smiled, a wide smile that curled one side of his mouth. It was perhaps a sarcastic smile, as if he read more into her remark than the obvious. She couldn't be sure. But all he said was, 'Good, then let's go forth.' He took a few steps across the room, opened the door, and ushered her, with a light pressure of his hand on her back, into the corridor. 'We'll start,' he said, 'in my own unit, the cardio-thoracic. I think that you will find it interesting.'

'I'm sure I will,' she murmured politely.

'We'll concentrate on the medical wards,' said Gregory. 'It's an ops day today, so the surgical wards are busy, and I usually confine myself to my own wards on my rounds, though in all spheres, but particularly this unit, surgery and medicine overlap constantly.'

They entered a short corridor opening off the longer one. 'This is the CT medical or long-stay department,' he explained.'Under the care of Sister Marie Jackson, a wonderful lady. She's going to be a difficult act to follow when she retires.'

Sister Jackson, a plump lady in her late fifties, made them welcome, and accompanied them round the series of four-bedded rooms that made up the unit. The walls of each room were festooned with an array of screens and equipment for monitoring hearts and lungs, blood-pressure, temperatures and a whole range of sophisticated information. But not all the beds or patients were plugged into them; in fact quite a few people were up and walking about, or sitting beside their beds.

'None of the patients in here are immediately post-operative,' explained Gregory. 'Post-op cases are cared for after surgery in our recovery ward. Compared to that, this unit is quite low tech. We have pre-op cases undergoing various tests or semi-convalescents in here. It's an important staging post before they go for surgery, or before going home.'

Erica was impressed by the way that Gregory greeted each person by name, and seemed familiar not only with their medical backgrounds, but with their personal history.

'How's your wife managing?' he asked one patient, Roger Heskith.

Fine,' replied Roger, 'now that she understands that when I come out I'll be virtually normal within a few weeks. Thanks for your help over that, Doc, and for arranging for someone to see her. It's just what she needed.'

When they left the wards, and sat drinking coffee in Sister's office, Erica asked for more information about Mr Heskith.

'He still looks rather frail, one can see that he's been very ill,' she said, 'and yet he seemed quite cheerful and optimistic, less anxious than one would expect of a patient recovering from a heart attack.'

'Well, he is still ill, but he's feeling better because of the treatment that he received following his coronary. Immediate and then the first few weeks' treatment are important following an attack, as you know. And yes, he is less anxious; his treatment and our efforts have reassured him. He was wildly fibrillating after his attack, and his heart rhythm was a mess, and that's the

condition that makes cardiac patients feel ill and frightened. But, with immediate treatment, the simplest —
that is aspirin and the drug streptokinase — his heart
settled down, and he's felt quicky reassured. By
explaining this to him and to his wife, we were able to
help them both. He'll go home, taking a daily aspirin
for the rest of his life, and informed about the right
sort of diet and exercise to take, and he and his whole
family will benefit.' He smiled at her. 'Of course,' he
said, 'it's not always as simple as that; Roger is one of
the lucky ones.'

'Yes, I realise that. I believe, though, that fatalities
from coronaries have been much reduced by these
comparatively simple methods.'

'That's true. Surprisingly it took quite a while and
many tests before this treatment became virtually the
established procedure that it now is. Immediate treatment and a defibrillator machine in most ambulances
have led to an enormous increase in lives saved, and
that gives us a chance to continue long-term restorative
treatment.'

'Do you think that, in addition to the purely physical
benefits of this treatment, the patient's less tense
psychological attitude has helped, because he suffered
less trauma at the outset?'

'Oh, without a doubt. Fear about taking exercise,
discomfort because of an arhythmic heartbeat, all took
their toll in the past. Now patients are more readily
reassured on account of the corrective treatment.'

'Quite,' said Erica. 'Reassurance plays a big part,
doesn't it, in recovery?' She swallowed the last of her
coffee, and thought about how alternative medicine
relied a great deal on patient response and faith.

Gregory looked hard at her, seeming to know what

she was thinking, his eyes probing hers, locking them into his.

He said, his voice low and serious, 'But that's not the end of the picture; it doesn't just rest with the patient's response. One needs expertise, years of training, to assess what is happening; anything else might be cruel, lethal and go dreadfully wrong. A lot of amateurs playing about at healing is to me a frightening prospect.' He stretched out a hand, and touched hers, lying in her lap, and his touch was warm and comforting. 'Erica, there's a lot more to curing people than just blind faith, you know; as a nurse you must appreciate that.' He sounded gentle and understanding, but firm; he was making a point.

Erica smiled at him, feeling for a moment, at least, on the same wavelength. 'Oh, I do,' she said quietly, 'appreciate that, but I'm also trying to keep an open mind. As I recall, not all medics went along with the current treatment for heart failure when it was first mooted. I just think that one shouldn't close one's mind to anything, especially where quality of life is concerned; it's not just surviving, but how one survives, which is important.'

She realised that neither of them had mentioned alternative medicine, but that that was what was uppermost in their thoughts. He was resisting being drawn even into thinking about it, and she was determined not to let an opportunity pass by which might give it credibility. If only she could make him see that she was not entirely sold on the idea, only anxious to give it a fair trial. She was just thinking how she might phrase this suggestion when he put down his coffee-cup, stood up, and suggested that they get on with the round.

'We've plenty of people to see yet,' he said, in a no

nonsense sort of voice. 'I like to show my face in each of the wards that I am responsible for, even if I can't speak to everyone, but it's a time-consuming task.'

Erica stood up at once, feeling slightly guilty for even contemplating delaying him by entering into a discussion.

Suddenly reminded what a caring doctor he was, she gave him a radiant smile, which lit up her whole face, and made her emerald-green eyes glow. It was quite spontaneous, but it was the sort of smile that generally knocked any man for six, and she couldn't help being aware of the fact. In this instance, she had no idea what sort of effect it might have on Gregory, and for a moment she didn't care. It was enough that she was with him. 'I'm ready when you are,' she said happily. 'And I'm most grateful to you for allowing me to tag along.'

Gregory gave her a rather quizzical sort of smile, and arched one eyebrow.

'I invited you, remember; you didn't twist my arm. I think that in your role as senior co-ordinator, and in order to do your job properly, you need to see as much of the hospital as possible, and understand its workings. I didn't approve of your appointment, but, now that you're here, the better informed you are, the more use you'll be to Princes, and that is my prime concern.'

'Oh, yes, of course,' said Erica, sounding cheerful, but feeling a little deflated. For a brief moment she wished that he wasn't quite so single-minded about her being beneficial to the hospital; it would have been nice if he'd indicated that he was enjoying her company for its own sake.

The next couple of hours passed in a blur of faces, places and information, as Gregory guided her round the many wards for which he was responsible, from the rehabilitation unit, which was being extended and nearing completion, to the oncology unit, where she met Ray Miller, the senior cancer consultant.

'What we're trying to do here,' he told Erica, 'is combine the workings of a specialist unit with a general hospital routine. Where possible, we follow the principles of the Bristol Cancer Help Centre, though we have to adapt to fit in with the fact that we don't have all specialist staff, but students doing part of their general training and so on. But we try to emulate the sort of care they give at Bristol, rather than stick to the more rigid hospital system. We think it works.'

'Ray Miller must be a wonderful doctor, and a very nice man,' said Erica, as she and Gregory left the unit, 'to be trying to do what he is with, as he explained, a shifting, untrained staff. People working in the cancer field really have to be dedicated.'

'Well, as he said, he's got a splendid support in his unit sister and the staff nurses, and some of his aide nurses have been with him a long time. It's just the students, both medical and nursing, who are floating. But they've got to learn their oncology care somewhere, and—who knows?—among those who pass through Ray's hands now may be our future specialist doctors and nurses. After all, Princes is first and foremost a general hospital, and it's our job to train people to fit the wider field of medicine, not just one specialist department.' He gave her a piercing look from his dark eyes, as if he expected her to argue with him.

He sounded just a little bit impatient, thought Erica, as if Ray Miller was lucky to have what he'd got, and should not be hankering for more. Or was it that he was somewhat distrustful of any innovative medicine?

Did he think perhaps, that even the approach to cancer should be limited to the totally conventional methods of a few years back? No, she couldn't believe that he could be so limited in his thinking. He was a highly intelligent and caring person.

She said in a conciliatory tone, 'Yes, of course, that's true — about having to look at the wider field. I must admit that I hadn't thought of that.'

She had been much impressed by the oncology unit and particularly by Ray Miller and his compassionate approach to his work, but it brought back bitter memories of her mother's final illness. She had been well cared for to the end by a team of nurses and doctors, and by Erica herself, but somehow Erica couldn't rid herself of the idea that she could have done more for her much loved parent. Common sense told her that it wasn't true, but she had to fight off a wave of sadness that threatened to engulf her, and which she was afraid she wouldn't be able to hide from Gregory if she let it get the better of her.

Squashing her sad thoughts, she said brightly, 'And thank you again, Gregory, for the tour. It's been most interesting. I'm grateful.'

He smiled down at her and nodded, his eyes compassionate, as if he'd guessed at her thoughts.

They were striding down one of the long glass corridors that connected all the units at ground level when the sun burst out of what had shortly before been a leaden sky, and shafted through the glass wall facing on to a small garden.

Gregory grasped Erica's arm.

'Let's go outside,' he said, in a stern and positive voice. 'It's time for lunch; we'll walk through the grounds to the refectory and get a breath of fresh air before eating.' He obviously assumed that they were lunching together, which she thought was rather high-handed. He hadn't mentioned the fact before, and she hadn't agreed. He didn't know, of course, that she had half promised Clare that she would meet her in the refectory at about twelve-thirty, so that they might lunch together and compare notes.

She opened her mouth to protest, but instead allowed herself to be ushered out through French doors into the mild spring sunshine. He kept his hand beneath her arm, and she realised that she liked the feeling of warmth and support that it transmitted. She hoped that he would keep it there. It made her feel cared for and protected.

She glanced up and sideways at him, just as he looked down at her. He smiled, and his whole face lit up.

He said softly, squeezing her arm gently, 'You're a very beautiful woman, Erica, and you have a warm and generous nature.' His smile widened. 'In spite of everything that I've said, I believe we're lucky to have you here at Princes.'

Erica didn't at first take in what he was saying, and, when she did, for one glorious moment she was bathed in a state of total euphoria. He had actually praised her, had admired her beauty and her temperament, and had looked and sounded as if he meant it. It was almost too good to be true. Her bubble of euphoria burst. It was too good to be true, at least on a personal level. He wasn't praising her for herself, but for what she might achieve for Princes. She was just another cog in his wheel to keep the hospital running smoothly. The last few words that he had uttered pounded in her mind. 'We're lucky to have you here at Princes'. That was all he thought about—his precious hospital; it blinded him to everything else.

He was the medical director of Princes Park, and that was really all that he cared about. It made him cautious where anything new was concerned, and it perhaps sometimes blinded him to wider issues, if they didn't exactly meet with his conservative approval. He wouldn't risk anything; that was why she would have to fight him on the alternative-medicine issue, and probably many more. He had spent the morning introducing her to his particular interests, and had almost brainwashed her into accepting his theories on practically every subject. Consciously or not, he had used his masculine magnetism to charm her into his way of thinking. Well, it might work on a lot of people, but not on her. She too had a job to do. She was going to be just as committed to Princes as he, but in her role as independent adviser to the committee, not as Gregory Hurst's mouthpiece.

Carefully she slipped her arm from his, and he didn't try to hold it. In an even voice she said, managing a little laugh, determined that he should not know how her mind had been working, 'Thank you for those kind words, Dr Hurst. I'll remember them. And thank you for the tour; it's been fascinating, but I'm afraid——'

Before she could finish her sentence, his bleeper sounded. He frowned heavily. 'Damn,' he said. 'I'm afraid I'll have to go to a phone. Wait here, I'll not be long.'

'Sorry, I can't wait. I have a luncheon appointment with Clare. See you later at the meeting.'

She made herself turn and start to walk away from him, although one part of her, in spite of her anger with him, didn't want to.

He caught her up in a few easy strides, and turned her to face him. 'I thought we were lunching together,' he said, and his eyes glinted dangerously.

'Yes, you thought we were, but you didn't ask me; you just presumed.'

To her fury, he started to grin. 'My dear girl,' he said, sounding amused, 'it seemed only natural, knowing that our visits would take us to lunchtime.' He grinned down at her, somehow making her feel that she was in the wrong. 'You didn't honestly expect me to abandon you, did you?'

She was able to say quite honestly, and in rather icy tones, 'I didn't give it any thought, Doctor.'

If she thought that her coolness would have any effect on him, she was mistaken. He said, still sounding amused, yet at the same time complimentary, 'Ah, of course, a beauty like you wouldn't, Erica. You don't have to work for invitations; they just fall into your lap.' He stared down at her hard, and she was conscious of being in full view of people passing by in the long glass corridor. She took a step backwards to put more space between her and the doctor, and stumbled on the grass bordering the gravel path.

Gregory put out both hands and grasped her shoulders. He was smiling broadly in an infuriating manner. 'Steady,' he murmured in his velvet deep voice. 'You mustn't fall over; you'd spoil the cool, untouchable image.'

Erica made herself look steadily back at him as she gently shook herself free from his grasp. In a distant, haughty voice she said, ' I don't go in for image-making, Doctor. I don't have to, I'm just myself.' She drew herself up to her full height and knew that she looked impressively dignified and composed. She was determined that he should not have the last word, or see her as a weak female who needed his support in any sense.

Gregory threw back his head and gave a shout of laughter. His eyes, his whole face, were alight with amusement, as if what she had said was very funny. He was about to say something when his bleeper sounded again, and he patted his pocket. 'It's no good, I must go, my dear, dear, spiky Miss Lang.' He stretched out a hand over the small space that divided them as they stood one each side of the gravel path, and lightly touched her cheek. 'Thank you for your delightful company this morning,' he said quietly, seriously, though his eyes still glinted with mirth. 'And for taking such an intelligent interest in everything. It's been a real pleasure having you along. Sorry about luncheon; another time, perhaps.'

Before Erica could reply, he turned on his heel and returned along the path through the door, and disappeared fast as he made his way to the nearest corridor phone.

For a moment she stood quite still, recovering from the genuine warmth of his words, and the touch of his fingers on her cheek. She could hardly believe that either had happened. Both his words and his gesture had been spontaneous and straightforward and honest, with no hint of sarcasm, or double meanings. His attitude gave her food for thought. She mulled it over as she stared down at the border of brilliant crocuses that lined the path. What would have happened, she wondered, if his bleeper hadn't sounded, if she had agreed to have lunch with him? Would they have entered a new and less contentious phase in their relationship? Would he have charmed her into being

influenced by him, or would her own beauty and ability
to fascinate have swayed him to her way of thinking?
His last few words to her, and his whole softened
attitude, betrayed the fact that he was not immune to
her beauty and intelligence.

With determination she shook off these unanswer-
able thoughts and then slowly turned and made her
way past the delicately scented beds of swaying daffodils and narcissi to the refectory and an uncompli-
cated luncheon with Clare.

CHAPTER SIX

AFTER lunching with Clare, and discussing the events of the round that she had made with Gregory, Erica went along to the pain clinic to keep her appointment with Larry Grey.

He was waiting for her when she arrived, looking rather subdued, his nice hazel eyes serious.

'Having asked you to come,' he said ruefully. 'I realise that there isn't much to show you, just a few cubicles, where I examine patients, and prescribe various pain-killers and conservative massage, if appropriate, or give people a bit of a pep talk, and, if they are willing and we've exhausted all the conventional methods, ask Mrs Bourne — Betty — if she can do anything for them.'

'Your faith-healer,' said Erica cheerfully, rather surprised to find Larry despondent after his enthusiasm on Sunday. 'I'd very much like to meet her if she's here. And surely it's because there are few "externals" to show for your work that you wanted me to see your department, and because you're aware that you often can't cure or even relieve pain by the usual methods that you're interested in alternative or complementary treatment. Surely you still want the committee to consider renting out the Dower House for that purpose; I can't believe you've changed your mind since yesterday.'

Larry brightened up, and looked more like the confident doctor who had approached her the previous day. 'Gregory didn't succeed, then, when he was showing you round this morning, in persuading you that if patients can't be treated conventionally they should not be treated at all.'

Erica felt herself rising to Gregory's defence, even though Larry had practically repeated what Gregory had said at one point.

'No, of course he didn't,' she said sharply. 'He didn't try. You know, Larry, his motives for taking the stand he does are as good as yours. It's not because he doesn't want patients to have all the help they can, but he feels it's cruel to offer hope where no hope exists.'

Larry looked at her speculatively. 'Oh, I don't doubt his integrity. But you, Erica, what do you believe?'

'As I said before, I'm neutral, but I think the whole matter should be open to discussion, and I'm willing to say so at the meeting.'

'Well, I must be grateful for that,' he said with one of his nice smiles. 'And I'll certainly help you get together a list of patients who have been helped by other than conventional treatment, though it will take a while to get together. And Erica, in case you should think otherwise, don't run away with the idea that I don't appreciate Gregory Hurst. He's a great guy, and a good director. We just don't see eye to eye on this issue, and he has so much clout that I feel somewhat defeated before I start, and there's always someone waiting to jump in on a dispute and cause trouble, sometimes just for the sake of it.'

Mrs Bourne appeared at that moment, and Erica had a short chat with her. She hadn't quite known what to expect, but certainly not this rather ordinary-looking, dumpy little lady carrying a plastic carrier-bag in one hand and an umbrella in the other. And yet she felt, after ten minutes' conversation with her, that there was something extraordinary about her, some sureness, some calmness that seemed to emanate from her. She couldn't put her finger on it, but it existed. She supposed that it was what was called an 'aura' in some circles.

The boardroom, on the second floor of the administrative block, was filling up fast when Erica arrived following her visit to the pain clinic. It was a low-ceilinged, elegant room, with a long table down its centre, set out with pads of paper, pens, pencils and water glasses and carafes. It had a businesslike air about it, like the boardroom of a merchant bank, or a similar high-flying establishment. Its formality was a little daunting. At first sight, Erica couldn't see herself contributing much to the meeting, especially if it turned out to be a powerful financial discussion, but she reminded herself that this committee on to which she had been co-opted was about policy as well as resources, and that was her forte.

She sat down near the foot of the table, where there were several empty chairs and from where she could survey the whole room. Gregory Hurst had not yet arrived, nor Clare, who had hoped to be at the meeting. Neither had the chairman, Sir Noel Barrington, but she recognised several other people whom she had met during the last week, or on previous visits to Princes. Most of them gave her friendly little nods of recognition or welcome, which she gratefully returned.

An elderly lady, with several wobbly chins and a shapeless felt hat pulled squarely over thick white hair, sat down beside her, patted her arm, and said in a booming voice. 'You're Miss Lang, if I'm not mis-

taken.' She proferred a hand. 'I'm Violet Hammel.'
She leaned towards Erica. 'Commonly thought to be a
bit batty.' She winked. 'But I'm quite harmless,' she
said with a broad smile. 'And my intentions are pure,
absolutely pure,' she added with a twinkle. 'I'm for
anything that's good for Princes.'

'Lady Violet,' said Erica, shaking her hand, liking
her at once, as she recalled Gregory's disparaging
remarks about her, and Clare's kindlier ones, on
Saturday afternoon in the cottage. 'I believe you're all
for selling off land for a leisure centre, and for renting
out the Dower House to alternative or complementary
healers, Lady Violet,' she said. 'You obviously think
that both moves would be a good thing for Princes.'

'Yes, I do, m'dear. We can spare the land, and the
expense of upkeep, and, as for renting out the Dower
House as suggested, well, it would be a good thing. I'm
all for holistic or any other medicine that will improve
a sick person's lot. I've seen acupuncture being used in
China, and seen it work. And I've got friends who
swear by herbal or homeopathic mixtures when more
conventional medication has failed or can't be toler-
ated.' She shrugged. 'My philosophy is that, if one
thing fails, try another. I can't see any harm in that.
Surely you agree, my dear.'

Erica felt herself being drawn to this old lady, and,
far from thinking her mad, thought that she was
eminently sensible, but she replied cautiously, 'Well,
it's not for me to say, Lady Violet; I'm only here to put
forward ideas suggested by other people, but I think
that some of the medical staff are against the idea of
this clinic because they're not sure that it is harmless,
psychologically if not physically.'

'Well, they can pick and choose who they let out

rooms to, and surely, having them under their noses, they can vet what they do. And it's not as if our doctors will be obliged to send patients to these alternative practitioners, but the choice is there if all else fails. The beauty of this arrangement would be that they are all under one roof, and Princes will be benefiting from the rents they're bringing in, and there's no reason why some patients at least should not benefit. That rent money, my dear, if you can get it over to the stick-in-the-mud medicos, will help fund some of our conventional needs, and nowadays no hospital can afford to ignore that.'

Erica, absorbed in her conversation with Lady Violet, suddenly became aware that Gregory was in the room. She didn't know how or why she was aware of him, but she just was. She didn't see him come in, but knew that he was there. It was uncanny. She raised her eyes and immediately met his. He was standing near the head of the table, listening to something being said to him by his next-door neighbour, but his eyes must have been on her all the time, willing her to look up, as indeed she had. He raised a hand, acknowledging her presence, and she nodded in reply. From thereafter, she was aware of his dominating presence, and his eyes on her much of the time. He might just as well have been sitting next to her and touching her, so conscious of him was she.

Lady Violet followed the direction of her eyes, and a smile hovered round her lips. 'Ah,' she said. 'Our esteemed medical director. May I ask if you have crossed swords with him yet?'

'We've skirmished.'

'A splendid man, but concern for his precious Princes makes him too cautious at times.' The elderly lady patted Erica's arm. 'But get him on your side and the battle's half won.'

Erica opened her mouth to repeat what she had already said about being neutral, but realised that it would do no good. In Lady Violet's book one was either for or against a project; there was no in between.

The chairman arrived and the meeting got under way. There were items on the agenda referring to the previous meeting, which Erica was not involved in, and then the floor was open for discussion of new business.

Several points of issue were raised before she had the chance to speak on behalf of Martin Blake, the kitchen supplies manager. She explained that he had need of new heated trolleys and put forward the suggestion that the co-ordinator of the League of Friends, who was present, might be interested in raising funds. Her suggestion was thought to be a good one, and put to the vote and accepted. And then she put forward the case for the physiotherapists, already stretched to the limit and knowing that more would be required of them when the extended casualty and rehabilitation departments were fully operational.

'I'm asking that provision should be made to fund at least one more physio,' she said, knowing that she was right to feel strongly about the issue. 'Otherwise the splendid effort made to raise funds for the enlargement of both these departments will be wasted.'

'I second that,' said Gregory's deep voice. 'We need an extra physio now for rehab, and at least another part-timer when the enlarged accident and emergency unit is going at full strength.'

Surprisingly, in spite of adverse murmurings from the financial experts present, the motion was carried, and it was agreed to employ the extra physiotherapists.

Erica couldn't believe her luck that her first two suggestions had been successful. How big a part Gregory had played in getting her request on behalf of the physios carried she wasn't sure, but she was certain that her next proposal, about the Dower House, would not be so well received. He had said that he would oppose it, and the most she could do was get a postponement of a decision while she sought for confirmation of patients helped by alternative or complementary medicine, as they had agreed.

In the event, she didn't have to put the issue to the committee, as Lady Violet did that, neatly dovetailing that proposal in with the proposal to sell off land for development.

'For both,' she exclaimed in her booming voice, 'are about income and not expenditure.'

It was a clever move, as the committee were divided about both measures, but not for the same reasons, and supporters for the one were not necessarily supporters for the other. It meant that Gregory was unable to rally his lobby against either project as a single objective.

Time was getting on, and the chairman suggested that both issues should be postponed and discussed at the next meeting in a fortnight's time. The motion was carried, and the meeting brought to an end.

Erica turned to Lady Violet as the meeting finished. 'That was clever of you,' she said admiringly, 'to link those two projects.'

'No good getting old if you don't get artful,' said that lady with a laugh. 'Gives us a breathing space to rally support for one or both issues. I know that Gregory plans to bring up the perennial question of more medical beds at the next meeting, and that means more building and more expenditure. Perhaps the idea of extra funds on the table might influence him about one or other of the projects. I'd like to see both get off the ground, but I'd settle for one for the time being—anything to boost our finances.'

Erica said, 'I can understand why Dr Hurst is opposed to the freelance healers' scheme, but why is he so against selling some land? Surely a few. . .' Her voice trailed off as Gregory Hurst strode up behind Lady Violet, who, seeing that Erica was looking with surprise at somebody over her shoulder, turned and looked up at him, a beaming smile on her plain, plump face.

'Ah, Gregory, fazed you that time, didn't I?' she said cheerfully.

To Erica's surprise, Gregory looked amused rather than angry. 'Lady Vi, you certainly did, bringing up both those two projects together,' he said easily. 'But then I'm used to being bested by you, cunning, charming lady that you are.' To Erica's further surprise, he bent over Lady Violet, lifted her hand to his lips, and kissed her fingers in an old-world if theatrical gesture.

Lady Violet reacted in kind. She patted him on the arm as if she might have held a fan. 'You're too charming for your own good, my boy,' she said, though with a pleased smile hovering round her mouth, 'just like your dear father. But you won't get past me that way, I intend to persuade you on this selling and renting issue, and I now have an ally.' She put a hand on Erica's sleeve.

To her annoyance, Erica felt herself blushing. 'I'm not exactly an ally, Lady Violet,' she tried to explain. 'I'm here to see fair play and put propositions to the committee on behalf of other people. I'm not rooting for myself.'

'Nonsense,' said Lady Violet. 'Whatever you say, I can see that you're keen on the holistic medicine idea. Anybody with a grain of sense would be.' She gave Gregory a challenging look, to which he replied with a wry smile.

'Would that it were so easy to reach a decision about this issue,' he said softly, his eyes on Erica. 'But I must be true to what I believe to be best for the patients, and nothing as yet has caused me to change my mind about the issue. I will not countenance a lot of quacks on the doorstep.'

'That's not fair,' Erica replied, her voice flaring into anger. 'Your colleague, Larry Grey, medically quali-fied like yourself, believes that some of it works some of the time. Do you know about Mrs Bourne? Have you met her?'

Gregory's lip curled in scorn. 'Larry's tame faith-healer?'

'Who else? Have you met her?'

He nodded his head. 'Briefly, a year or so back. Nice enough lady, but I wasn't impressed medically speak-ing. Of course I accept Larry's word that she has helped patients he couldn't do anything for. But this happens all the time in conventional medicine. A good nurse, a suddenly correct diagnosis, a sudden chemical upsurge in a patient's response to medication, all can be responsible for a dramatic improvement that seems little short of miraculous. Any doctor with a fund of experience will tell you the same.'

'So you wouldn't accept a case history indicating that something unusual had happened after a patient had received all possible conventional treatment but had eventually responded to unconventional healing?'

'I didn't say that. I'm still prepared to look at properly documented cases.'

Erica turned away from him and began gathering up her papers that were lying on the table, and tucking them into her briefcase. 'Good,' she said starkly, feeling almost unreasonably angry with him for being so cautious, so conventional. 'I'm glad about that, Dr Hurst, because I plan to have several such cases ready for you in a fortnight's time.'

She closed her briefcase with a snap, and prepared to move away, and only then noticed that she and Gregory were the last two people left in the room. At some point Lady Violet, whom she vaguely remembered seeing getting into conversation with someone else, must have slipped away, and then, like everyone else, left the room.

She raised her eyes to meet Gregory's again, and found him, to her surprise, smiling. He stretched out a large hand. 'Truce,' he said. 'To be sealed with a drink in the refectory. It's well after six, and I feel like packing up for the day, so how about it, Miss Lang? Shall we drink to a friendly, if turbulent, future in our efforts for Princes?'

His smile, showing large, gleaming white teeth, was wide and reassuring, and his words, uttered in his deep voice, honest and convincing. He was not only devastatingly handsome, but mature and self-assured. It gave her a glowing feeling in the pit of her stomach when he smiled. She had the feeling that he would know exactly what to do to make a woman feel happy and fulfilled, if he so wished.

She stopped a blush rising to her cheeks, as her

imagination took flight at the idea, but couldn't prevent a shiver of pleasure running up her spine in anticipation of spending some time in his company. Her hand, as she touched his, trembled slightly. He was having a remarkable effect on her, making her heart beat faster, and her legs feel shaky, an effect that she had not experienced since her first overwhelming love-affair in her early teens. Since then, until now, she had had no difficulty in keeping a tight rein on her senses in her relationships with men, always remaining in control of them and herself. Some sixth sense told her now that if she began what might be a pleasurable affair with Gregory Hurst it would be he, and not she, who would be in control.

Well, so what?

She looked up at him through long lashes, assessing him and her unexpected reaction to him, not sure for a moment how she wanted to proceed with this strong-willed man. She was aware, without being deliberately seductive, that her emerald-green eyes were probably looking even more brilliant than usual, on account of the conflicting emotions that were chasing themselves round her mind.

It gave her a glow of satisfaction when she heard his sharp intake of breath, and knew that she was affecting him to some degree, and perhaps even as much as he was affecting her. And so she should, she thought suddenly, her normal confidence where men were concerned returning. She too had looks, sophistication and presence, why should she not affect him as he did her? Probably for him, too, being bowled over by the opposite sex was something that rarely happened, or that he allowed to happen. He must be in the enviable position of having the pick of the field to choose from when it came to women; maybe he even found it a bit of a bore having women fall for him too readily. Maybe, she thought with an inward smile, he might even enjoy a challenge from a woman prepared to hold her own.

As Gregory's hand closed over hers, Erica took control of herself, and returned his handshake firmly. 'Yes,' she said, in a steady voice. 'Let's call a truce, and I'd love to have a drink with you, Dr Hurst.'

His hand tightened slightly before he released it. 'Gregory,' he reminded her. Then, 'Splendid,' he said. 'Let's repair to the refectory.'

Erica stood up and together they walked to the door, which he held open as she passed through, and her shoulder brushed against his chest. Another small tremor of pleasure rippled over her. She smiled up happily at him, determined to put aside the antipathy that his reactionary response to the two schemes for raising money for Princes caused. She was looking forward to spending an hour in his company on a personal level, and she hoped that he felt the same.

She was sure that he did when he bent his head and murmured, 'I wish we could make it dinner at Poachers, or somewhere more intimate, instead of drinks in the refectory, but alas, I have a date that I can't break.' His eyes gleamed and a rueful smile lit up his handsome features. He seemed genuinely regretful.

Fleetingly, she resented the woman with whom he was having dinner, and for some reason she had no doubt that it was a woman. 'So have I,' she replied in a cool, matter-of-fact voice, 'a date.' But she didn't reveal that it was a homely meal to which she had been invited by her secretary, Kate Gentry, who wanted her to meet her husband and family. Let him imagine what he would — that she was being squired by a masculine charmer — just as she was picturing him dining with a svelte beauty.

He took her arm as they emerged from the admin building and started to walk across to the Old House and the refectory. She might have resented it from some men as being too intimate, too possessive on such a short acquaintance, but, strangely enough, she didn't feel that with Gregory. It seemed a comfortable, companionable gesture, and, in spite of her turbulent reaction to him earlier, when he had touched her, curiously without sexual overtones. The sun had not long set, and because the sky was swept clean by the March winds that had been blowing on and off all day there were still remnants of colour in the west; faint strawberry, and a delicate aquamarine streaked across the pine-clad hills of the horizon. The sky to the east was a dusky purple with a dusting of pale stars. The wind had dropped.

'A perfect spring evening,' said Gregory, sniffing appreciatively as they passed the beds of daffodils and narcissi bordering the path connecting the two old buildings at the very heart of Princes Park.

'Yes, as a newcomer, I'm finding Princes full of magic. There's something about this place that affects one the minute one walks into it. It has to do with vitality, and friendship, and a history of caring.' Erica wondered if she sounded too effusive, insincere, which was the last thing that she wanted to do. It was just that this particular moment in time, with the scents of the spring evening all about her, it seemed right to speak honestly of her feelings. She finished apologetically, 'I don't mean to sound fulsome, but there is something — an aura — that is special to here.'

'There is indeed,' replied Gregory, seeming pleased and unsurprised by her outburst. 'Princes Park is special. We like to think that it has more to offer than any other hospital of its size and importance. It isn't a faceless entity, but a family concern, and all who work here, in whatever capacity, are family. I think you'll find that that is how the most prosaic of us feels, although we may not be very good at saying so.'

They reached the heavy oak door of the Old House, and Gregory pushed it wide open and ushered her through in front of him. A great pile of logs was burning in the fireplace, behind a brass fender, sending leaping, flickering shadows across the unlit hall. The scent of hyacinths was almost overwhelming, deep and vibrant as the colours that they displayed.

It was, thought Erica, like coming home to a warm, loving welcome, and with Gregory at her elbow the feeling was complete. In spite of their differences, and his autocratic manner, he was part of the ambience, the essence of goodwill that seemed to flourish at Princes.

She gave a sigh of pure pleasure as they crossed the polished floor of the hall on their way to the refectory. It was all so perfect. A rumble of voices met them as Gregory opened the door and found places for them in a corner booth at the bar end of the room.

He leaned on the table as she sat down, fingers splayed out as they supported his arms and massive shoulders. A scattering of hairs on the backs of his well kept hands curled blackly against the pristine white cuffs of his shirt, protruding from his jacket sleeves. 'Was that a happy or sad sigh that you've just given?' he asked softly, eyebrows raised questioningly.

'Oh, happy,' she said. 'Definitely happy.' She smiled

up at him. He was in such a gentle mood that she wanted to explain how she was feeling at that moment, sure that he would understand and not think her silly and sentimental. 'I was just thinking that I'm really beginning to feel at home here. The fire, the flowers. . .' she faltered '. . .you and I.' She opened her hands eloquently, palms up. 'I don't know quite how to explain it; it's just a wonderful, warm feeling of belonging.'

Gregory gave her a long, slow smile. 'In spite of our differences?'

'In spite of our differences.'

He nodded and straightened up. 'Good. Now what are you going to drink, my dear?'

'A white wine with soda, please. I shall be driving later, so I mustn't have anything too strong.'

'Ah, yes, your date. You're not being collected, then?'

It was half a question, half a statement. For a moment she was tempted to tell him where she was going for dinner, but some mischievous or perhaps cautious streak persuaded her to let him go on thinking that she had a significant date with a man. She shook her head. 'I choose to go under my own steam,' she said, and lowered her head so that he wouldn't see the fun dancing in her eyes at her innocent deception.

'Of course,' he said with a hint of amusement in his voice, as if he might almost have guessed what she was concealing. 'What else would an independent lady like you do?' His mouth quirked at the corner. 'I'll fetch our drinks; I won't be a minute.' He turned on his heel, his rugged physique and confident bearing marking him out as a figure of authority as he made his way to the bar. Even the back of his head, with its well cut shock of wiry black hair, seemed to Erica authoritative and dignified. It was hard to believe that anything or anyone could deceive him, even in fun.

She was left with the feeling that he had turned the tables on her, and had won that round of good-natured teasing, though how, she wasn't quite sure. Not that she minded, she realised, as she waited for him to return; she was feeling mellow and quietly content with her day. Without doubt she would enjoy her drink with Gregory, and equally enjoy her meal with Kate and family later.

A sigh of satisfaction escaped her as the sense of 'belonging' that had enfolded her in the hall hit her afresh. It was a wonderful feeling. What a lovely end to a busy and interesting day, in which she had met the redoubtable Lady Violet, and won a couple of victories at her first important meeting. It didn't matter that she still had future battles to wage against Gregory Hurst; at this moment in time she was simply relaxed and happy, and at peace with him and the rest of the world.

The feeling of blissful contentment was with her when she awoke the next morning as memories of the previous evening drifted through her mind.

Her drinks interlude with Gregory had been delightful, in spite of the fact that they'd continued to talk shop for part of the time, and even argue as they had at the meeting. Everything had been touched with a kind of special ambience that she couldn't pin down, however prosaic their conversation.

'What do you think of Lady Vi?' he had asked with a wry smile, as he set their drinks on the table.

'I think she's a very astute old lady, not batty, or potty, as you called her. In fact she's a darling.'

'Of course she is,' he agreed. 'I'm very fond of her — fond enough to hurl the occasional insult her way — and she does likewise, I may say. We have a sort of running feud going.'

'Yes, so I gathered from what she said. I also gathered that she knew your father; how come?'

His answer surprised her. 'My father was a founding member of Princes Park as you see it today. He was the godson of the original owners, whose family had lived here for centuries. He inherited part of the property, and bought out the others who had inherited with him. As a doctor, and with help from people like Lady Vi and her family, he set up the hospital.'

'Does that explain why you are against selling off some land for development?'

'Yes. My father was all for hanging on to the assets.'

'Times change; he might think differently now.'

Gregory looked at her, his dark eyes luminous. 'I know,' he said. 'But I'd heard so many stories from my father about the holidays he spent here as a child. I suppose I don't want to see anything change, and I am by no means sure that selling off is an advantage.'

She said gently, finding it rather touching that memories of his father should be affecting his judgement, 'Perhaps you should listen to impartial observers; their opinion might help. You're too close to the problem.'

He grinned in a way that made her heart turn over. 'Are you trying to influence me, Miss Lang?' he asked softly.

Erica shook her head, and returned his smile. 'I have no opinion at all on this,' she said. 'I only know that Princes, like any hospital, can do with more funds.'

'And your precious healers' clinic, bringing in rent, how do you feel about that?'

'That it should be given a hearing, as I have already said.' To her surprise, she found herself stretching out across the table to stroke the back of his hand, sensing that he needed comfort. It was a bold and involuntary gesture that seemed so right. He turned his hand over and caught hold of hers, imprisoning it in a strong grasp.

'No more than that? You're not personally involved?' His voice for a moment was quite harsh.

She shook her head, surprised by his vehemence. 'No, I'm neither for nor against it; I know very little about it.'

'Good.' He smiled and released her hand.

They talked a little longer, and then parted, each to keep their dinner date. Courteously Gregory escorted her to the foot of the stairs in the hall before saying goodbye. 'We must do this again soon,' he said softly, and touched her cheek. 'We need to get to know each other both on and off the battlefield,' he added with a quirky grin.

'I'd like that,' she replied simply, as she turned to mount the stairs. She stopped on the first-floor balcony that ran round the hall, and looked down. Gregory was still standing there at the foot of the stairs, the silver hair at his temples glinting in the subdued lighting. He lifted a hand in farewell as she started up the second flight of steps to the turret flat.

'Goodnight, my dear,' he called out quietly. 'See you tomorrow.'

This parting promise had completed her wonderful feeling of contentment, and, recalling this now, as she scrambled out of bed, she experienced a wave of elation. In a few hours she would see Gregory again. It was ridiculous to feel so exhilarated by the thought,

but she was. It was a fact. Her usual common sense
deserted her as she hugged the blissful thought to
herself and showered and dressed, and made ready for
the day ahead.

CHAPTER SEVEN

'WHAT a fool I was,' Erica muttered to herself for the umpteenth time, as she jogged briskly along the gravel path round the main hospital buildings, 'to imagine that he meant it when he said that he wanted to see me again. What a joke. So he had to go away in a hurry, but surely he could have got in touch since. There is such a thing as a telephone, even in the wilds of Scotland.'

So they had only known each other a short time; so he hadn't fixed a date proper with her! But they had both known when they'd parted on that Monday evening, that there was something special going on between them. Or had it all been on her side? Thoughts and doubts like these had been going round and round in her head for over a week. With a great effort and years of training behind her, she had prevented them from intruding on her work, but when, as now, her mind was free to wander, it persisted in coming up with all sorts of ideas about what was keeping him, Gregory, silent.

It was ten days since her drinks interlude with him, and she'd learned when she'd arrived at her office the following morning that he had been called to Scotland on some urgent business. It seemed that he was frequently being called to Scotland. Clare, who had endorsed this information that Kate Gentry had given Erica, seemed rather tight-lipped about the matter, and reluctant to say much.

'Gregory's got a strong sense of duty,' she'd said when explaining his absence. 'He has commitments that he can't avoid, and there's always someone ready to take advantage of him.' She had given Erica rather a bleak smile. 'But there, he knows what he's about, and can take care of himself. I just hope that he's not away too long. He may not be, as the saying goes, indispensable, but at the very least Princes misses him.'

And not only Princes, thought Erica grimly, breaking into a little burst of speed to relieve her feelings; it was incredible how much she missed him, and she'd barely known the man a week. It was ridiculous to feel hurt because he hadn't contacted her, because he had no obligation to her whatsoever, but she did.

She turned the corner from the north end of the buildings and started down the long, straight stretch that ran from north to south. It was nearly the end of March, and a typical south-westerly wind blew vigorously into her face, strong enough to stir up dust and fine gravel. Her eyes began to water, and she blinked several times to clear them. The wind howled up the passageway formed by the path running between the tall buildings on one side and a high bank on the other. It was unpleasant and hard work fighting against the wind, and she almost gave up and slowed to a walk when a few spots of rain hit her hard in the face. But she concentrated on keeping going, and tried to stop thinking about Gregory. Head down, she thrust herself forward against the fierce gusts of wind.

She was about halfway along the narrow path, where the bank was at shoulder-height, when she heard a sound coming from behind and above her, a sound that she couldn't identify, mingling with the buffeting of the wind as it did, but which seemed like something between a shriek and a shout and the tinny ringing of a bell.

Still jogging, she half turned to see what it was, and had a vague impression of a bicycle being ridden unsteadily along the edge of the bank by a blurred figure. It was coming fast, and seemed to be wobbling, out of control, skimming off the bank almost on top of her. Instinctively she turned her head away, and ducked. She felt a terrific and painful thump as the full weight of something crashed into and over her back and right shoulder, the force twirling her to one side, just missing her bent head, and throwing her against the wall. She slid down the wall, feeling the rough brickwork grazing her face and knees, as the machine sailed on through the air and hit the path in front of her, swerving from side to side before flinging the rider off and careering away down the track.

For a moment she lay winded in a crumpled heap, barely taking in what had happened. Slowly her senses returned. She lifted her head cautiously, and gave a gasp of pain as the movement reached her right shoulder. She breathed in deeply several times as she realised that it was injured where the bike had struck her; but at least she could move her head, which seemed undamaged apart from being sore where she had grazed it against the wall. She tried raising her head again, focusing her eyes on the body of the rider of the bicycle, who was lying very still, a few metres ahead of her. Was he unconscious? Had he hit his head and knocked himself out when his bike swerved?

Erica cleared her throat, and brushed some fine gravel away from her lips. 'Hi,' she called. 'Are you all right?'

There was no response from the prone figure. She

could see now that it was a young boy of perhaps ten or eleven, with a shock of blond hair. There was a cut on his forehead that was bleeding profusely; his face was ashen. He really did look very still indeed. Her tummy churned with fear. How badly was he injured? She must get to him and examine him, for there wasn't a soul about, and unlikely to be at this time of the morning in this part of the grounds, unless somebody else was out jogging. She looked up and down the empty track, and up at the windowless lower walls of the basement of the building. No one would be able to see them at an angle from the higher windows. She must stand up and look over the bank and across the field, to where a drive ran parallel to the path from north to south, and attract the attention of the driver of a passing car. Relief flooded over her. She wouldn't be alone for long; she could get help. Staff would be coming to work soon; somebody would see her if she shouted and waved. Meanwhile she must try to get to the boy and see if she could do anything for him.

She started to stand up, keeping her injured right arm and shoulder still, using her left hand as a lever against the wall. An excruciating pain that made her cry out shot from her right ankle, through her calf to her knee. It was agony. She lay panting with pain for a moment, trying to work out how to move. Obviously her ankle and leg were damaged, perhaps broken. No, not broken; surely the force of the bike hitting her shoulder couldn't have done that. Her leg must just be badly twisted. She would have to crawl along the path; no way was she going to be able to stand.

A wave of pain from her shoulder washed over her, and she felt sick and faint. She mustn't faint. She took a few deep breaths, and felt slightly better. Now she would try to reach the boy, who was still not moving. The foot of the path, where it turned round the south side of the building and joined the concourse and car park in front of the hospital, was about thirty metres further on. If she could, she would make for there after looking at the boy. There would be plenty of people about and she could get help. She gritted her teeth, and slowly began to drag herself along the gravel, fighting down the waves of nausea that washed over her as shafts of pain all down her right side attacked her. Even her left ankle hurt, she realised, as she levered herself with her left hand and arm, the only limbs that seemed quite unaffected by the accident.

At last she reached the prone body of the boy, just as he stirred and groaned. 'Thank God,' said Erica, managing a small reassuring smile as the boy opened puzzled eyes. 'You'll be all right. Just lie still; don't try to move.'

'What. . .where?' He lifted his head slightly, and Erica saw with relief that his eyes focused properly and the pupils looks normal and equal, with no sign of deep concussion. Just the same, he mustn't move until she got help, in case there was internal damage. She repeated that he mustn't move. 'It's important,' she said firmly. 'I'm a nurse and I know about these things. Promise me you won't move till I get back with help.'

The boy closed his eyes. 'Promise,' he muttered, and then mumbled something about his head, obviously aware of the cut on his forehead.

With difficulty Erica pulled a clean tissue from her tracksuit pocket, and mopped some of the blood from his face, and then left the tissue stuck over the wound, hoping it might stem the flow a little.

By this time she felt sick again and faint with pain,

and it took all her courage to start the long crawl towards the end of the path. All her right side felt as if it were raw and on fire, and her left ankle felt as if it might burst at any moment, and she knew that it must be dreadfully swollen.

After she had crawled what seemed to be miles, she raised her head to see how much further she had to go, and cried out with frustration when she saw what little progress she had made. 'For God's sake,' she said out loud through clenched teeth, to give herself courage, 'you can make it,' and, determined not to give in, gave a great heave forward. She was aware of a blinding flash of pain as her injured side scraped along the gravel, and at the same time saw a figure in a tracksuit appear at the bottom of the path. She could have wept with relief. 'Here,' she called, and waved her good arm, ignoring the intense pain that was engulfing her.

The tall, broad figure spurted up the slope, and in a second was kneeling beside her.

Erica stared up at him through a veil of tears of pain. 'But Gregory,' she gasped, 'you're in Scotland,' and then she passed out in a dead faint.

When she came to, Gregory was crouching beside her, taking her temporal pulse. She opened her eyes wide. 'The boy,' she mumbled.

'He's OK, I've looked at him. No sign of concussion or internal bleeding that I can detect.' He sounded dry, matter-of-fact. 'I'm more concerned about you; you've been out for several minutes, time enough for me to get help. The ambulance will be here any moment.' Another wave of pain passed over her and she felt herself drifting away. The relief of having Gregory there was wonderful, and she didn't have to worry about the boy. She just wanted to sleep. 'Look at me,

Erica,' said Gregory's voice sharply. She blinked and looked at him vaguely, and he studied her eyes intently, and then nodded. 'Good,' he said, 'nothing wrong there, pupils fine. He held up his hand and splayed some fingers. 'How many?' he asked.

She wished that he wouldn't press her; she wanted to sleep. 'Three,' she mumbled. She shifted her position a little, and was at once overwhelmed with such pain that she cried out.

'Tell me where it hurts most,' said Gregory.

'Side, right shoulder and right leg. Left ankle. Pain's awful.' Her lips would hardly move — even they felt stiff with pain — and her voice was a whisper.

'I'll give you something for that as soon as the ambulance arrives.' There was the sound of voices and feet on the gravel path, and Gregory's voice answering, but she couldn't distinguish the words all the time. She heard him say something like 'little scratch', and then the pain began to recede, and there was blissful oblivion.

Over the next hour or so she kept surfacing, but only just. It was rather like being in a half-asleep, half-awake state. She was conscious of going to the X-ray department and of being in a cubicle in Casualty, and of Gregory being present; and then she was given another shot of pethidine while the simple dislocation of her left shoulder was reduced by manipulation, and reality slipped away again.

When she was reasonably alert, Luke Steel, the clever accident and emergency consultant, gently explained the situation. 'Gregory and I examined you,' he said, 'while you were partly sedated, and we were able to reduce the dislocation relatively easily. And now that your shoulder is immobilised it shouldn't give you too much trouble. You've been X-rayed, and there are no fractures, thank God. But I'm afraid you're going to have quite a bit of pain on account of the mass of torn ligaments and tendons in your shoulder, back and right leg. There's already considerable discolouration and effusion into the joints. Only time, massage and pain-killers are going to help that condition. And your left ankle, too, is badly sprained and must be rested, so my dear Erica, you'll be out of action for a couple of weeks or so. Gregory will be looking after you as he's senior staff consultant. He'll be planning and supervising your day-to-day treatment. He's just arranging for you to be admitted to a room in the private wing; he'll be back any moment.'

'Two weeks? I can't believe it. Surely it's not as bad as all that,' Erica said in a high voice, unlike her usual low tones. She felt near to tears, not because of the pain so much, though it was fierce, but because she felt so helpless, trussed up in a mass of bandages, and wearing a shapeless hospital gown. In addition to her arm being in a sling, there were bandages round her chest, hip and leg. And, though slight, the grazes on her face worried her; they felt sore and ugly and disfiguring. The thought that Gregory had seen her looking like this, and probably worse when he had first examined her, was humiliating, and the thought that he was going to be looking after her for two weeks even more so. She would be entirely in his hands, and she had no doubt that he would use his medical authority to the limit when treating her, and he wouldn't countenance any shorts cuts to recovery.

He entered the cubicle at that moment, and stood beside Luke Steel. He gave her a wry, sympathetic smile. Whether he had heard her outburst, she didn't know, but, as always with him, she felt that he understood more than he should about what was going on in her mind, and his smile almost seemed to convey as much. 'Well, my dear,' he said quietly,'you have been in the wars. We'll get you fit as soon as possible, but you'll need some patience while these ligaments are healing; you'll be pretty inactive and uncomfortable, I'm afraid.'

Through the miasma of pain, shock and sedation, Erica, her mind wandering in a dreamy state, thought how handsome these two men were, as they stood at the foot of the cubicle bed and surveyed her. Princes was lucky to have such clever, dedicated doctors, her sentimental, uncontrolled throughts rambled on. There wasn't a lot to choose between them for sheer good looks, she considered hazily, as the last shot of pain-killer began to get to work, but Gregory, though slightly older, had the edge on Luke, and he was so. . .so. . . On this incomplete thought, she drifted into sleep again.

When she woke, though she kept her eyes closed as she orientated herself, she was immediately alert, much more her usual self. Her muddled, tearful state seemed to have disappeared in her sleep, the side-effects of the drugs having evidently worn off. She recalled the details of the accident, and experimentally tried to turn her head, and experienced a shaft of intense pain in her neck. It was so unexpected that she gave a small, gasping scream, and then froze, afraid to move again.

Across the room, a chair creaked, and footsteps came towards the bed. Cautiously Erica opened her eyes, and saw Gregory smiling down at her.

'Ah,' he said softly. 'Awake at last, and evidently in pain.'

'Only when I move,' she panted. 'If I lie still——'

'You'll get stiff and stuck,' said Gregory with a chuckle. 'So we'll see about more pain-killers shortly. I've written you up for some hefty doses over the next few hours. I don't want you to suffer needlessly; there's no reason why you should. Don't try to be stoical. Let me help you all I can.'

He was so kind that Erica felt the tears, which she had thought behind her, welling up afresh. She blinked to dispel them, and coughed a little, which hurt like hell. She winced, and compressed her lips. 'I don't want to be dopey all the time,' she said with all the firmness she could muster.

'Tch, tch, Miss Lang, arguing with your physician already; it's not allowed, you know.' His voice was full of humour as he gently teased her.

'I feel such a fool,' she murmured, 'lying here with just insignificant injuries. It isn't as if I've been in a bad crash.'

'My dear girl, that's precisely what you have been in. The fact that it was just a bike has nothing to do with it. You were hit at such an angle that the full force of the boy and machine striking your right side resulted in extensive injuries. Not life-threatening, but severe enough in their own way, and only rest and conservative treatment will help at this moment.'

Erica, only too conscious of feeling sore and helpless, knew that he was right. 'OK,' she said with the traces of a smile. 'I'll try to be a model patient.'

'Good girl. Now I'm going to give you another injection which will relax you and help the pain, and then get a nurse in to help you freshen up and change out of this.' He flicked at the starched hospital gown with a strong finger. 'Clare called in earlier with a few of your own things from your flat. She was sure that you wouldn't mind her foraging for them, that you'd appreciate having them.'

'Oh, I do. God bless Clare for thinking of it.'

There was a receiver and syringe by her bed, and Gregory drew up an injection and administered it into her left upper arm. 'There,' he said, as he swabbed it over. 'That'll make you more comfortable for an hour or so, and able to make minimal movements.' He turned and made for the door, and Erica wanted to cry out to him not to go, for, almost against her will, she felt so safe when he was near by. At the door he paused. 'I'll be back later to say goodnight,' he said, with a gentle smile, as if perhaps he knew what she was thinking. 'Meanwhile, I'll send a nurse in to make you your usual beautiful self.'

'Fat chance of that,' she replied, making an enormous effort to be humorous and touching the grazed areas on her cheek with her good left hand. 'I must look a mess.'

Gregory took a step back towards the bed. 'A beautiful mess,' he said. 'Make no mistake about that.' And he turned and left the room.

In the few minutes that it took for the nurse to arrive Erica looked, as much as her painful neck would allow, around her. She was in a large, comfortable, well furnished room, with picture windows looking out across the parkland. She recognised it as the *en-suite* in the private wing, a delightful room, normally reserved for VIP patients. What on earth was she doing here? There were perfectly good side-wards for staff, where she could have been nursed, off one of the medical or surgical wards. So why here?

A nurse came in at that moment. She introduced herself as Staff Nurse Lee, who was to special her.

'But I don't need specialling,' said Erica in dismay. 'I'm not totally helpless, though I could do with some help to wash and change, and go to the loo.' She smiled at the pleasant-looking staff nurse. 'No offence, Staff, but I don't need round-the-clock surveillance.'

'Then you'd better tell that to Dr Hurst and Sister Adams, Miss Lang,' said the staff nurse cheerfully but firmly. 'When I'm on duty, I'm to special you. Orders is orders, ma'am,' she said with a laugh, clicking her heels together and giving Erica a mock-salute.

Erica thought, I'm going to like her. Out loud she said, 'It's Erica, please, not Miss Lang. Hell, that makes me feel so ancient.'

Staff Nurse Lee looked pleased. 'And I'm Lizzie,' she said, holding out her left hand so that she could shake Erica's good hand. They shook hands. 'Now what can I do to help?' she asked. 'Shall I get a wheelchair to take you to the bathroom, or would you prefer a bedpan and a bed wash?'

'What do you think?' said Erica. 'Just get me some wheels and give me a hand as necessary, and I'll manage.'

'Strict instructions that you're not to put any weight on your right foot, and only limited use of your left,' said Lizzie. 'Or you'll get me hung.'

'Well, I don't want to do that,' replied Erica. 'But with your help I think we can obey the rules, and I can wash and change in a semi-civilised manner.'

'You're on,' said Lizzie. 'Though I'm getting some-one else to help get you out of bed; between the three

of us we'll manage.' She went off to fetch the wheelchair and another nurse.

It took Erica half an hour and a lot of help from
Lizzie to get washed and changed into her own night
clothes. But it was worth it, she thought, as she
eventually collapsed exhausted on the bed, feeling
halfway human in her ivory silk pyjamas with wide
legs, and a loose tunic top. At least she looked and felt
reasonable, with her mahogany hair brushed into its
usual neat, collar-length bob by Lizzie, and a spray of
her favourite perfume masking the antiseptic that had
been used on her dressings. But she was exhausted,
and hoped that if Gregory was returning, as he had
said, it would be soon.

It was dusk now, and Lizzie wanted to close the
curtains, but Erica stopped her. 'It's nice to look out
and see the lights across the park,' she said, 'and see
the last of the sunset and the stars beginning to come
out.'

Very romantic,' said Lizzie. 'Now can I get you
anything else? You've fruit juice and water on your
left-side table, if you're sure you can manage.'

'Thanks, I'll be fine.'

'I'll be in the office; ring if you want anything.'

'Will do.'

She dozed on and off for most of the evening,
refusing supper, but drinking copiously. Lizzie, after
introducing the night staff nurse, went off duty at eight,
and Erica almost gave up hope of seeing Gregory again
that evening. She was bitterly disappointed, and cross
with herself for being so. After all, the poor man had
other patients to see, she reminded herself, and he'd
already given her more attention than he strictly
needed to. He need not for instance have stayed with

her over the afternoon to be around when she woke up, but he had stayed, and she must be grateful for that.

Night Sister made her rounds just before ten o'clock, commiserated with her on her accident, and reminded her that she was written up for pain-killers and sedation and not to be afraid to ask for either. Clinging to the faint possibility that Gregory might yet call to see her, and wanting to be alert if he did, she gritted her teeth against returning pain, and refused medication for the time being.

She dimmed her bedhead light, and lay back against the mound of pillows, staring out at the window full of glittering stars. It was a cold, frosty night. The March wind that had bothered her that morning had dropped, leaving the night sky a clear dark indigo. It was, as Staff Nurse Lee had said, a romantic night.

Romantic? seethed Erica. There's nothing romantic about looking the way I do, black and blue all over, and most of it seen by the one man who matters to me. How ridiculous, to feel the way I do about a man for the first time ever, and end up like this. . . The first time ever! Her heart jolted to a sudden standstill, and then thundered away painfully in her chest, which felt tight and restricted, but not only by the bandage. She struggled to steady her breathing. What do I mean, she asked herself, the first time ever, the way I feel about this man? How do I feel about him?

You're in love with him, said a breathless voice in the back of her head. You've fallen madly, utterly and painfully in love with him. But I've only known him for a few weeks. . . So what has time ever had to do with falling blindly in love? But we fight about all sorts of matters, and I think he's arrogant and blinkered about

many things. How can I be in love with him? Because
he's a wonderful doctor, and kind and gentle to his
patients, and now you're a patient, and he's been kind
and gentle to you. . . Except that he hasn't come back
to say goodnight as he said he would; if he was that
wonderful, he wouldn't have forgotten.

Angrily she brushed away a large hot tear of frustration, and self-pity, and sadness, which trickled down
her sore cheek. She felt silly. 'This,' she whispered into
the dim room, 'is madness, and I mustn't let him know
how I feel. It must be all on my side, or he would have
got in touch with me when he was in Scotland, and
he'd certainly have come back to see me tonight.'

There was a knock at the door, and it opened slowly,
and Gregory's large, broad form stood silhouetted
against the light in the corridor. 'Hi,' he said softly.
'I'm sorry I'm so late, had a bit of a crisis on.' He stood
in the doorway, clearly waiting for her to invite him in.
It was nice touch, when he had every right as her
doctor to come in at any time.

Erica caught her breath, and lied airily, 'It's all right,
I didn't really expect you. I guessed you'd be busy. Do
come in.'

He crossed from the door in a few easy strides. 'I
thought you might be asleep,' he said.

'I seem to have been sleeping for most of the day.'

'Shock,' he said succinctly. 'And pain. Takes its toll,
makes one tired.'

'Nature's way of telling one to ease up.'

'Exactly.'

She was breathless with the pleasure of seeing him,
but some devil made her say, her words coming out in
a rush so that he wouldn't divine her feelings, 'Holistic

care, that's what you're talking about really, which is what——'

He didn't let her finish, but put a finger to her lips, and sat on the edge of her bed, taking hold of her good left hand. 'Don't let's quarrel; it's the last thing I want to do with you,' he said softly. 'I've had enough shocks for one day, finding you so dreadfully battered on the track.' He squeezed her hand gently. 'You gave me such a fright.'

The thought that he had been frightened was immensely pleasing. She could just see his luminous dark eyes in the dimly lit room, and saw that they were full of compassion and understanding. They were not distant, or black or cold, as they could sometimes be, but full of warmth and light. He turned her hand over, and stroked her palm with his thumb, sending tremors of nerve-racking delight trickling through her.

She tried, half-heartedly, to draw her hand from his, but he simply tightened his hold. 'Don't fight me all the time, Erica,' he said softly. 'There's no need. I think that we're both aware that we're attracted to each other, and your accident today has highlighted that. Do we need to pretend to be distant with each other?'

As so often before in the brief period that she had known him, she felt that Gregory could almost read her mind. How else did he know what she had only just admitted to herself—that she was in love with him? And yet that was what he was implying. He had used the milk-and-water phrase, 'We're attracted to each other', but his smouldering look, and the tone of his voice, implied more than that. It had said as plainly as if he had said the words, 'I know you are in love with me', and he was all but admitting that he was in love with her. But could he be? For if he was, how could he go off on his jaunt to Scotland without a word? Her poor tired mind tried to grapple with the problem.

The situation now seemed as unreal to her as the proverbial Scottish mist, she thought with a hint of tired humour. True, Gregory was here, he was holding her hand—that was real enough—but what he was saying seemed odd, at variance with what she knew of him as a man. She was sure that he was not the sort of man to go around hinting at love, as he just had. He was a practical, down-to-earth, scientific man, not given to poetic fantasies; he liked his facts to be obvious, and capable of being proven. His opposition to the healers' clinic was proof enough of that. But there seemed, beneath the hard man of science and fact, a softer man, a more vulnerable person, who had been drawn to her as she had been drawn to him.

If only she could be sure of his feelings; if only he hadn't gone off to Scotland without a word. She mustn't let him know the depths of her feelings for him, that was certain. Not yet. Besides, they might go away. She didn't understand them herself. She had never found herself in this position before; men had adored her, and to date she had never returned their deeper feelings, or felt at a loss. Perhaps it was just because she was in pain and tired, and Gregory was her doctor, that she felt the way she did. For didn't everyone fall in love with their doctor?

All these thoughts winged their way through her mind as Gregory sat on the side of the bed and continued to slowly and rhythmically stroke the palm and wrist of her left hand.

As if divining her thoughts yet again, he said softly,

'Don't worry about it now; just rest and go to sleep. We'll talk more tomorrow; everything will seem clearer in the morning.' He bent a little closer. 'I'm going to give you another injection, and you are going to sleep like a baby.' His voice was infinitely deep and soothing, and suddenly all she wanted to do was sleep.

'Promise?' she asked faintly.

'Promise,' he said firmly, and slowly he raised her hand to his lips, and then released it and stood up.

Erica felt her eyes drooping even as she heard him pick up the syringe from the receiver on her bedside locker. From a great distance she heard his velvet voice say reassuringly, 'Just a little scratch. . .' and then Gregory and the room faded into oblivion.

CHAPTER EIGHT

For Erica the next few days passed in a blur of visitors, pain and intermittent relief from pain following injections and soothing massage from the physiotherapist. The physio's visits, though, were a mixed blessing, a blend of relief and torment; while massage soothed, coughing exercises to keep her sore chest free from infection were hell.

'It's the torn ligaments,' said Gregory, rather formally, calling the day after her accident with his registrar and houseman on his official round. 'They're going to be jolly painful for a bit, until they heal. That's why you must be sensible about taking pain-killers as prescribed.' His mouth quirked at the corners. 'However much that goes against the grain.' He knew, of course, that she was unlikely to argue with him in front of his junior colleagues, even though she disliked the idea of taking a lot of medication.

In spite of her pain and discomfort, she managed a smile in return for his, and couldn't resist saying, knowing that he would get the double meaning, 'Of course I wouldn't dream of going against your orders, Doctor, and I think in my case strong pain-killers are a necessary treatment at this moment; it's conventional medicine at its best. But don't you think that there are occasions when one might look for an alternative?' Her green eyes were open wide. She was the picture of innocence.

He understood that she was teasing him, and his

deep-set dark eyes gleamed with humour, but he said in a firm voice, 'Not for my patients, my dear; I like to use methods that I can trust. I'm sure you understand, don't you?' One well marked eyebrow was raised questioningly.

'Of course,' she said sweetly, 'perfectly,' knowing that he meant that he was still dead set against the idea of the clinic. In spite of the fact that his personal attitude was softening towards her, and surely her hazy memories of last night confirmed this, he hadn't changed his ideas about the clinic; he was as antagonistic as ever.

But this little spurt of rebellion with Gregory didn't last. She really felt too battered for the next few days to worry much about the clinic, or any of her other work. Amazingly, she was content to lie resting most of the time, and to doze or talk quietly to her succession of visitors, who included her secretary Kate, Clare Dunn and, most evenings, Gregory.

When he came in the evenings he was wearing his other hat, as friend rather than doctor, and, apart from asking how she was in a general fashion, he didn't discuss her treatment or medication. Neither were there any moments of intimacy such as had occurred that first evening. Gregory seemed not so much aloof as determined to keep their relationship on a purely friendly basis. Perhaps he felt that it would be taking advantage of her in her weakened state to pursue a more intimate line, for he made no more allusions to the special quality of their infant relationship.

For her part, Erica was content to leave matters in his hands, and not proceed any faster. She loved his visits, and made the most of them, simply enjoying his presence. As before when they had socialised, they talked about all manner of things, or rather, because Erica still tired quickly, Gregory did most of the talking, allowing her to draw him out about his work in general, and Princes Park and his commitment to it in particular. She would have liked to draw him out about his other commitment in Scotland, but wasn't successful, until Sunday, the fourth night of her convalescence, when he disclosed a little about his reasons for his trips there.

By now she was feeling more her usual self. The restricting bandage around her chest, which had been applied to support her dislocated and inflamed shoulder, had been removed, and she was wearing a simple sling. Her right leg was feeling less painful, and she could partially weight bear on her sprained left ankle, now encased in a strong support bandage. With the aid of an elbow crutch she could move about her room, and, blessed relief, take herself to and from the bathroom.

When Gregory arrived for his evening visit she was sitting in an armchair in the window embrasure, looking out over the park, which was beginning to fade into the April dusk. Another armchair was drawn up at the other side of the window, and a low coffee-table, on which stood a slender vase of long-stemmed red roses, stood between the two chairs. The deep window embrasure gave views to the south, east and west, and the orange and flame colours of the western sky, where the sun had just set, illuminated Erica as she turned and smiled at him.

Gregory stood quite still for a moment, reluctant to disturb the picture that she made as she turned towards him, the radiance of her smile. She must, he thought, be pleased to see him. A surge of pure pleasure engulfed him at the thought. It had been years since he'd allowed a woman to so affect him; any liaisons he had formed had been, on his part, honest but temporary affairs to fit in with his work, concluded without hurt to either side. All the women whom he had squired around had been beauties of a sort, but none had attracted him as the gorgeous Erica did, and it wasn't her skin-deep beauty that enthralled him, but her lovely, natural manner, her enthusiasm and intelligence, her determination. These qualities set her apart.

Her mahogany brown hair glinted fire in the reddish glow from the sky, and her green eyes seemed more emerald than ever, brilliant.

He returned her smile across the width of the room, and Erica caught her breath. He looked marvellous, she thought, so elegantly casual and masculine, in a stone-washed, heather-coloured blouson suede jacket, over a slightly paler cashmere sweater. His grey wool trousers were tailored to perfection, revealing muscled thighs and calves. He looked so strongly masculine that he took her breath away. She *was* pleased to see him. Her heart beat an uneven tattoo. It is as well, she thought tartly, that my torn ligaments are on the mend, or they'd never stand it. Her smile widened at the nonsensical thought.

'Evening,' she said, her voice slightly husky. 'It's lovely to see you.'

Gregory gave a little half-bow. 'My pleasure,' he said in his deep voice, which gave her yet another jolt. He had the most beautiful cultured tones, vibrant, but capable of being soft too, soft and gentle. She'd heard that he had a splendid singing voice, and could quite believe it. He would be a baritone, she guessed, a light baritone. 'It's good to see you up,' he added, although since he'd given permission it obviously hadn't come as a surprise to him.

'I've been watching the sun set. It was magnificent tonight, all pinks, purples and oranges.'

'Yes, so I noticed as I walked up from the Small House. A wonderful sight; all that April rain-washed sky made the colours brilliant, artists' palette stuff,' he said cheerfully, and, to her surprise, unselfconsciously. She wouldn't have thought him capable of such a poetic allusion. It showed how little she really knew of him, she thought a little sadly, feeling that she would dearly like to know more.

But in addition to his surprising remarks about the sunset, she had noted his reference to the Small House. That too was a surprise, as until now he had seemed unwilling to speak about where he lived, and she had only recently heard it mentioned by Clare.

'The Small House; that's your home, isn't it?' she asked, hoping she didn't sound too direct, too inquisitive, not wanting to give the impression that she had pried into his private life.

'Yes, it is. It was left to me by my father. He inherited it quite independently of Princes Park. It stands on the boundaries of the park.'

'I see. No wonder you don't want to see any changes made here.'

He crossed the room, and stood looking down at her, his expression enigmatic. 'Only changes for the better,' he said.

Erica felt challenged. She ignored the sensation that his nearness was having on her, and said, 'And you, I suppose, are the only person who knows what the best is?'

He stared down at her, swallowing his disappointment, knowing that he had been about to kiss her, not get into an argument with her.

'I think that I have Princes' reputation at heart as much as — perhaps better than — many. Believe me, I have no personal axe to grind, unlike some.'

All at once, Erica realised that they were heading for another of their confrontations — a confrontation that she didn't want. She bit back an angry retort, and regained her calm. He wasn't likely to give in, so she would have to. In fact she wanted to. After all, perhaps he was right; perhaps he did know what was best for Princes. He'd been associated with it for a hell of a long time; that must give him some sort of advantage.

She put out a hand and touched his arm, looking up at him appealingly. 'I'm so sorry,' she said softly. 'I don't mean to be pushy. You must think me very bold, as a newcomer, taking a stand against you.'

Gregory put a warm hand over hers. 'Erica, as you told me yourself not long ago, it's your job. I wouldn't expect anything else of you, but perhaps we ought to draw up lines of demarcation, and try not to mix business with pleasure.'

'It'll be hard not to have any shop talk; we're both so involved with our work.'

'Let's keep it general, then, not specific.'

'Agreed.'

They smiled at each other, suddenly and delightfully completely in accord, and, after giving her hand a small squeeze, Gregory relinquished it and sat down in the armchair at the other side of the window. He sighed contentedly, stretched out his long legs in front of him, and clasped his hands behind the back of his head. He looked completely relaxed.

He glanced at the roses on the table between them.

'Lovely flowers,' he said. 'Roses in springtime, makes a change from the ever abundant daffodils at this time of year.' He turned his head and looked at her, but Erica couldn't see his face as he had his back to the sky-bright window. 'You obviously had a visitor today.' He quirked a grin at her. 'An admirer, perhaps?' There was a faint question in his words.

'Larry Grey, not exactly an admirer, simply a grateful client.' In spite of her innocent words, she found herself blushing.

'Red roses from a grateful client?' Again the questioning tone was there as he looked at her quizzically.

Erica nodded. 'Larry's *very* grateful,' she said blandly, suppressing a smile.

Gregory asked her directly, 'Is he important to you?'

She would have resented the question from anyone else, but Gregory's impersonal directness made it inoffensive. He seemed genuinely interested, but in a distant fashion. For a brief moment she found herself wishing that he was less distant, perhaps even perturbed by Larry's obviously more than grateful interest in her. Well, she thought, with a little burst of defiance and pride, not wishing to reveal her own growing interest in him, if he can be enigmatic, so can I.

She shrugged non-committally. 'As I said, he's just pleased to have my support, and he's fun to be with, and we seem to understand each other well.'

Gregory looked at her rather sombrely. 'That doesn't exactly answer my question, does it, as to whether Larry is important to you?'

This time Erica was annoyed. He sounded less impersonal, more pressing. Quite at variance with her wishful thinking of moments before, she now resented his more personal approach. What right had he to

question her about her affairs in this manner? No rights
at all. She was not going to give anything away. If he
was genuinely interested in her, let him say so; she was
damned if she was going to lay herself open to his
mature charms. If there was any truth in what he had
said about a special relationship developing between
them, let him be the first to put himself on the line.
What a pity that they were again rubbing each other
up the wrong way. It was sad. She had thought that
tonight was going to be different, that they were not
going to argue all the time, but would get to know each
other better. Only minutes ago they had agreed to put
their antagonism over hospital matters on hold, but
now they seemed to have replaced it by a prickly
personal response to each other. Gregory appeared to
think it perfectly all right to grill her about whatever
he wished, and yet still be cagey aboout his own affairs.
Well, if he could question her about Larry, why
shouldn't she question him about his 'Scottish
commitment'?

Anger made her say stiffly, 'Do you always give your
patients and senior staff the third degree about their
personal affairs, Dr Hurst? How would you like it if I
did the same to you?'

If she had hoped to shake him by the formality of
her address and her suggestion, she was disappointed.
He looked at her long and steadily for a few moments,
a half-smile hovering round his lips. Her gaze faltered
beneath his, and she lowered her eyes. He unclasped
his hands from behind his head and pushed back the
coffee-table with the red roses on, and leaned across
the small space it left between the chairs. He extended
his hand.

'Come,' he said. 'Give me your hand.' Almost

mesmerised, she stretched out her hand and let him take it. He pressed it gently. 'Don't let's quarrel, Erica,' he said softly. 'Don't let's fight over this. I'm prepared to be an open book to you.'

'Really?' Her voice was full of disbelief. She gazed at him wonderingly. Did he mean it? Would he tell her all that she wanted to know about Scotland if she asked? Nobody, with perhaps the exception of Clare Dunn, seemed to know anything about his Scottish connections. Even the grapevine was short of hard facts, though rumours were rife. So would he tell her all, if she asked? 'Then tell me about Scotland,' she said, 'and why you have to visit there so often.'

He looked genuinely surprised. 'Scotland?' he queried vaguely. 'What has Scotland to do with Princes Park?'

'As much as my relationship with Larry has to do with it,' returned Erica sharply.

'*Touché*.' He inclined his head, and his mobile mouth quirked again at the corners. 'It seems,' he said, with a deep chuckle, 'that I am hoist with my own petard, but I've made the offer of frankness, so I'm all yours, Miss Lang; interrogate as you please.'

His willingness to be frank was rather overwhelming. 'Will you have a drink first?' asked Eica, relieved to be able to play the hostess for a few moments, and get back on to familiar territory. 'My secretary arranged for the fridge to be stocked up,' she explained, waving her hand towards the walnut cabinet that concealed a drinks fridge, as in the best hotels, another touch of luxury in this private suite, 'as I seem to be having any number of visitors.'

'I could murder a pink gin,' said Gregory. He let go of her hand and stood up. 'Shall I do the honours?'

'Please.'

'And you'll have?'

'A Perrier water, please. I don't think my doctor would allow me anything else while I'm on medication.'

'No,' he said with a laugh, 'I don't suppose he would.' He moved over to the drinks cabinet and poured their drinks. 'Ice and lemon in yours to make it look civilised.' He rattled the glass so that the ice clinked invitingly, and then, as she took the glass from him touched her glass with his. 'To us,' he said, 'and frankness.'

'To frankness,' replied Erica.

Gregory raised his eyebrows. 'Not "to us"?' he queried, noticing the omission, his eyes dark, commanding, wanting an answer.

Erica almost gave way beneath his gaze, but was determined to keep control of her senses. She pushed down the desire to drown in the look that he was giving her, and to confirm his 'To us' enthusiastically. But she was conscious that she must stand her ground with this powerful man, and not yield too readily. 'Perhaps, after we've talked,' she said cryptically.

'And I've coughed up my innermost secrets?'

'Exactly.'

'Right, you wanted to know why I have to whisk off to Scotland every five minutes,' he said expressionlessly.

Suddenly Erica felt very uncomfortable. It had been a terribly impertinent question to ask, considering she had known him such a short time. His private life had nothing to do with her, and even the fact that he'd questioned her about Larry didn't excuse her.

She felt the blood rush to her cheeks as she turned to look him full in the face. 'I'm so sorry,' she said quietly. 'Forget that I asked; it was dreadfully rude of me. My apologies.'

There was a moment's silence, and then Gregory said, 'But I started it, asking you about Larry. I don't regret it, and I'd still like to know how meaningful your friendship is with him.'

He stood up suddenly, abruptly, and moved across the small space between the chairs to stand looking down at her. He twirled the glass with the pale pink remains of his drink between his strong fingers. 'As for Scotland,' he shrugged, 'it's family business that takes me there. A close friend who was also a distant relative died last year, a cousin many times removed. His widow needs help with his affairs. It really is as simple as that.'

'Oh, I see, I'm sorry.' There wasn't anything else to say. It was, on the surface, simple, as he'd said, but she did wonder whether this widow was the somebody who Clare had suggested was taking advantage of him. After all, it was strange that the sort of affairs that needed his attention should be triggered off by an emergency call in the early hours of the morning, which was what had apparently precipitated his last trip to Scotland. Was it only concern for his widowed relative that sent him haring off when she called, or was there some other reason? After all, he'd said that the man who'd died was a close friend as well as a relative, which implied that he was of a similar age, which also meant that his widow might be quite young and beautiful. Was this the attraction?

Gregory was still there, staring down at her. 'So what about Larry? Does he begin to figure large in your life, Erica?'

'Well, hardly, as we're only just getting to know each other, but I like him very much.'

'How much is very much?'

A little leap of anger, tinged perhaps with jealousy on account of what she had just learned of his Scottish connection, again possessed her at his probing question. She said tartly, 'I should think about as much as your distant relative by marriage means to you, if what you have said is true.'

Gregory went very still for a moment, and then asked in a harsh voice, 'What have you heard about Helen and me?'

Erica was startled. 'Well, n-nothing,' she stammered. 'Nobody knows anything about your affairs. I only know what you've just told me. I didn't even know that your relative was called Helen.'

'Really? Not even over our famous grapevine?'

'Not even over that.'

There was a few moments' silence, and then he said softly, 'I'm glad about that; I wouldn't want you, of all people, to get a garbled version of the situation.'

His words warmed her a little, but she still sounded rather stiff as she said. 'Then perhaps you should tell me yourself, if there's anything to tell.'

He said sternly, 'There's nothing to tell, but tongues will wag. Helen and I ——'

The telephone shrilled; the receiver was beside the bed.

Gregory began to walk towards it. 'Shall I answer for you?' he asked.

Erica nodded. 'Please.'

He picked up the instrument and listened, and then turned to Erica. 'I'm afraid it's for me,' he said. 'I had to leave your number; we've an emergency brewing.'

She shook her head. 'It doesn't matter,' she said.

He was several minutes on the phone before the call finished.

'I'm sorry,' he said, as he put down the receiver. 'I'm needed in the unit. Unexpectedly, we've heard from another hospital that a possibly suitable heart and lung donor has come up, and we've hopefully a suitable recipient whom I have to help assess for surgery. Teamwork, you know.'

'I understand,' said Erica. 'Please go. There's obviously some urgency about the situation.'

'It's good of you to understand.'

'Why, I am a nurse, you know, as well as a co-ordinator. I know that in these sort of situations everyone has to be prepared for immediate action, so please go.'

'Will do.' To her surprise, he bent down, and swiftly kissed her on the lips, but it was a paternal rather than a lover-like kiss. 'Wish us luck,' he said. 'We always need it in cases like this.'

She returned his kiss, her breath coming and going, fast and unevenly, but he didn't seem to notice. She guessed that his mind was already on the job ahead, and nothing else mattered. 'Good luck,' she whispered.

He walked towards the door. 'Thank you,' he said. He turned to look at her. 'I'm sorry the evening had to end this way.'

'It goes with the territory,' she said.

'Yes, that's true.' He raised a hand in salute. 'See you,' he said, as he let himself out of the room.

'See you,' she echoed.

The room seemed very empty after he'd gone, leaving behind him only a whiff of his astringent cologne. But his solid, broad-shouldered image remained in her mind—large dependable, very male—and she could still picture his dark eyes peering down at her, and see the silver flashes in his black hair, and feel his cool lips on hers. He had kissed her without passion, and yet it was an important kiss, a kiss of friendship. It was rather touching, she thought, that he had followed this with a request to wish him luck. As the man of science that he was proud to be, luck seemed too vague a commodity to ask for, though maybe even the hard, exacting science of applied medicine, like everything else in life, needed an element of luck to make it work.

Luck and faith, she mused, as she sat on in the armchair and watched dusk turn into a deeper twilight as the sunny April day turned into night. The room darkened, but she was lost in thought, and hardly noticed. Her mind was half with Gregory, preparing to assess a patient for a life-saving operation, and half with tomorrow's meeting of the policy and resources committee. It was the meeting at which she had promised to come up with six confirmed cases of cures by complementary or alternative medical practitioners. Well, she wouldn't be there now; she wasn't fit enough to attend, and, in any case, she had only collected five cases. Gregory had every right under the terms of their agreement to refuse to discuss further the plans for renting out the Dower House. He could have the whole thing squashed, unless Lady Violet came up with an idea.

Oh, well, thought Erica a while later, getting painfully to her feet and making her way to her bed, it's in the lap of the gods now, what happens at tomorrow's meeting. I'll just have to accept the decision that is made, as a question of luck. I've done what I can.

On this thought she eventually fell asleep, her mind busy with the events of the evening, and what might have been, had Gregory not been called away. Would they have got closer? Would his chaste kiss have been warmer, or would they have continued to find matters to argue about, either personal or work-orientated? She had no idea. They just seemed to strike sparks off each other whenever they met.

She was awoken in the morning by a tapping at her door. 'Come in,' she called, and opened her eyes, expecting to see one of the duty nurses bringing in her early morning tea.

It wasn't a nurse but Gregory who appeared, carrying a tray with two cups and saucers on it.

'Morning,' he said cheerfully. 'I waylaid the nurse, and begged a second cup. I hope you don't mind.'

Automatically Erica put up a hand to smooth her hair. She must look a mess, having just woken up.

Gregory took hold of her hand. 'Don't,' he said. 'You look lovely, all tousled with sleep.'

She felt herself blushing, but managed to say in an even voice, 'You're taking an unfair advantage of me, Doctor, doing a round this early in the morning.'

Gregory made an explosive sound in his throat. 'Dammit,' he said forcefully. 'This isn't an official visit, but a friendly one, following on from last night. I thought that you'd like to know that the transplant is going ahead OK. The surgeons are still working.'

Erica took a sip of her tea, and found that her left hand was shaking a little. 'That's marvellous,' she said. 'So both donor and recipient were compatible.'

'Yes, as far as we can tell.'

'You must be pleased.'

'Pleased, relieved. My chap hadn't any future without an almost immediate transplant. In fact it's a miracle that he's kept going as long as he has.'

'I suppose that your palliative treatment and faith and hope has keep him going.'

'That's right, and, I have to admit, mainly the latter.' Gregory walked over to the window, and paced up and down. 'Apparently a friend who is a faith-healer was bolstering him up before he was readmitted to us.'

'And?'

'He derived a lot of comfort from what she said and did. She seemed to have made his condition more bearable. At least that's what he says. Of course he must have had one of these slight remissions too, which nobody can account for. Anyway, with one thing and another, it was enough to make him hang in there while waiting for a transplant.'

'I'm glad that it gave him time for you to do your stuff,' she said softly. 'He might have given up without that sort of back-up.'

'Yes,' said Gregory briskly. 'I suppose he might.' He turned and looked at her, sitting up in bed looking, as he had said, tousled, but lovely. Her green eyes were glowing with understanding, and some other emotion that he couldn't pin down, and her mahogany-brown hair shone like silk. He had never been so moved by a woman. He turned away from her again, and moved back to the window area, saying, as he stood with his back to the light, so that she couldn't see the expression on his face, 'I thought it only fair that you should know about this case. It makes no basic difference to how I feel about non-conventional-type medicine, but I do think that the committee should have a chance to debate the issue, and for this reason will withdraw my opposition to future discussion.'

'Oh, Gregory, thank you, that's marvellous.' Erica's voice was soft and warm with surprise and pleasure. 'I was wondering how today's debate would go. I suppose,' she added wistfully, 'there's no chance of you allowing me to attend?'

'None whatever, my dear girl, you only tried out the elbow crutch yesterday, and stayed out of bed for any length of time then. You're still a mass of torn ligaments and bruised muscles, and only time and rest will heal those. You'll be fit for the meeting in a fortnight's time. You must be patient till then. Meanwhile you can start doing some work from here with your secretary's help. Make the most of that.' He swallowed the last of his tea. 'I must away now, the unit's going to be busy today, but I'll try to pop in again this evening.' He bent over the bed and brushed his lips across her forehead. 'Goodbye, have a good day.' He put a large, gentle hand on her good shoulder and squeezed it tenderly, and looked down at her for a long moment, his dark eyes looking velvet-soft.

'Goodbye,' she whispered as her eyes met his. 'I'll look forward to this evening; I do hope you can come.'

'You know,' he said in his low, vibrant voice, 'that I'll do my level best.' Then he strode towards the door and let himself out without a backward glance.

The sight of Gregory's broad shoulders as he exited from her room that Monday morning was the last that she saw of him till Thursday, when he visited briefly on an official morning round.

Erica was appalled at how tired he looked. He was drained and exhausted, and his deep-set eyes had become sunken and hooded. She had heard that he had been frantically busy since Monday, dealing with some sort of virus that was raging through the cardio-thoracic unit. As if that wasn't enough for him to deal with, she had just learned from Clare that the heart and lung transplant patient was showing signs of rejection. Poor Gregory, he couldn't have been faced with more difficulties, she thought, eyeing him with concern as he examined her and congratulated her on her improvement.

'You'll be able to manage the stairs to your flat in about a week's time,' he said, with a professional, rather forced smile, obviously shrugging off his tiredness to do his job. 'And get to your office,' he added.

'Good, I'll look forward to that.' She was as formal as he, though she wanted to put out her hand and touch his, and tell him that she understood that he was tired and dispirited and anxious. She felt that he needed an encouraging word, but now was not the time. If only he could relax for half an hour, as he had last Sunday evening, stretched out in the armchair admiring the April twilight. She took her courage in both hands, not sure how he would receive the suggestion she was about to make, but knowing that she would have to risk his response. 'There is something that I would like to discuss with you,' she said, as he and his entourage were about to leave. 'But it's a private matter. Would it be possible to see you later?'

Gregory stared down at her with his tired, sunken eyes, which still managed to hold a knowing, sardonic gleam, as if he had guessed at her thoughts.

A world-weary, rather cynical smile quirked at one side of his mouth. 'I'll try to visit this evening,' he said. 'But don't bank on it.'

His registrar and houseman were at the door. Erica
raised her eyes, full of compassion and understanding.
'Just try,' she said softly. 'Just try.'

It was ten-fifteen when he arrived in her room. If he
had looked tired that morning, he looked infinitely
more exhausted now, as he sank into the armchair that
had been turned round to face the bed.

'I shall probably drop off,' he warned apologetically.
'I'm not very alert, but fire away if you have something
that you wish to ask me.'

Erica blushed a little. 'That was a ruse, I'm afraid,
to get you to come tonight. I've no problems, I just
thought that you needed a break from work. You have
finished for the night, I take it.'

Gregory nodded. 'If all goes well. I think we've
managed to reverse the rejection in our heart-lung
chap, and the virus seems at last under some sort of
control.' He didn't seem surprised by her confession
that she had nothing to discuss with him.

There's a pink gin on the table beside you,' said
Erica softly. 'I thought that if you weren't working it
would relax you.'

'Ah, the co-ordinator-cum-trouble-shooter is seduc-
ing me with hard drink,' said Gregory, raking up a
tired smile.

'That's the idea,' said Erica cheerfully, suddenly
feeling her usual competent self. 'My role is to assist
all staff, however exalted.'

'And I need assistance?'

'You need an ear, a sounding-board.'

'To unload some of my problems?'

'To share the load.'

'My dear girl, Erica, I've never needed to "share the

load", as you put it; I've always been quite capable of dealing with matters on my own.'

'That I can believe, but I thought that perhaps a sympathetic ear. . .?'

'Your ear, my dear, will do at any time,' said Gregory. 'Sympathetic or otherwise. Had you anything in mind?'

'No.'

'Well, I have. What about dining with me, say, a week from tomorrow—Friday—to sort out our difference of opinion on my needs and yours? You'll be ready for discharge by then. In fact you can go back to your flat on Thursday, back to the daily grind of fighting other people's battles. So what about it, Erica, will you come out to dinner with me?'

'I should love to.'

'Put on your glad rags; this is going to be something special.'

'I shall look forward to it.'

He left soon afterwards, not kissing her this time, just going away with a quiet goodnight.

CHAPTER NINE

THE following week flew by for Erica, in spite of the fact that she saw little of Gregory. He made a couple of official visits and called in briefly on several evenings unofficially, but to some deegree the latter weren't very satisfactory. One evening he had Clare with him, and on the other occasions she already had visitors with her, so their meetings were social and superficial. Erica wasn't sure whether she was glad or sorry that she and Gregory were denied the opportunity to talk more intimately, and she couldn't guess how he felt about it. His demeanour gave nothing away. In fact she half wondered if he was deliberately avoiding seeing her on her own while she was still a patient, and was content to wait till their dinner date to further their relationship.

She made good progress physically. On Thursday she returned to her flat, limping a little still, and using a stick, but with both legs working virtually normally she was able to make it up the stairs to her turret. She was still having physio to her back and shoulder to relieve the stiffness and tissue congestion, but her bruises had faded to a marbled khaki, and she was feeling remarkably fit.

Friday was a red-letter day, for it was the day that she was to have dinner with Gregory, and it also marked the day of her return to her office proper. For although she had been working over the past week from her room in the private wing, and was quite up to date with her work, it was lovely to feel back in the thick of things and be able to deal with people face to face.

Her first interview was with Jack Lennards, the head porter, who had left her the cryptic message about car parking weeks before. He was a tall, thin, grey-haired, bespectacled man with a large moustache, who had worked at Princes Park for longer than anyone could remember.

He sat opposite Erica at her desk on Friday morning, stroking his moustache as he explained his problem. 'It's the visitors' subsidiary car park,' he said. 'Not only is it too far from the main buildings, but half of it's waterlogged after a good shower. And who gets all the brickbats from the visitors? Well, we do — me and my men; we're the first in the firing line, so to speak. I've mentioned it to all the VIPs time and again, but nobody takes any notice; it goes in one ear and out the other. But it ain't fair to the visitors, especially the old ones, having to tramp all that way, and it ain't good for Princes' image, a car park like that. First impressions,' he finished gloomily, 'are very important.'

'But they have got a nearer car park, haven't they, which is divided between the staff and visitors?'

'It's nowhere near big enough now, not with all the extending we've done over the last few years; and that's when they started the makeshift second park, to accommodate the extra visitors. It was supposed to be temporary till they extended the original parking area, but it ain't worked out like that; everyone's forgotten about it being temporary.'

'Except you, Jack,' said Erica cheerfully. 'Thank goodness you've kept it in mind. I'll certainly bring it

up in committee on Monday, and see if we can get
something moving.'

'You mean that, Miss Lang? You really will bring it
up?'

'Of course, that's what I'm here for.'

'You don't need any more convincing, then, that we
need nearer parking? I can easily show you, if you like
to come and look.'

'No, that won't be necessary. I parked there the first
time I came for an interview, and I was surprised at
how far from the hospital it was, but I assumed that
the nearer car park was bigger than it is, and that most
visitors could park there. And of course I didn't know
anything about it flooding; that's an additional reason
to get something done about it, and the fact that we're
still extending the rehabilitation unit, and Casualty,
which means more patients and even more visitors in
the near future.'

Jack Lennards stood up and offered a large, work-
roughened hand across the desk. 'Well, miss, I never
thought that you'd get my meaning so quick; I thought
that you'd think that I was only grousing, like. Thanks
very much.'

'That's what I'm here for — for people to grouse to,
among other things — and yours is certainly a legitimate
grouse.'

'Great, I'll say goodbye, then, and thanks again.'

As the day progressed, Erica found it more and more
difficult to keep her mind on her work as she anticipated with growing pleasure the prospect of dinner
with Gregory. There was a great glow inside her that
wouldn't be quelled. It would be wonderful to be alone
with him, and away from Princes, even, she thought
with a glimmer of trepidation, if they argued all the

time. After a month of working and being hospitalised following her accident within the hospital boundaries, she was ready for a change of scene.

She wondered where he was going to take her. 'Put on your glad rags,' he'd said, so perhaps it was going to be somewhere rather grand. On the other hand it might be some bright night spot; she had no way of knowing.

When she eventually arrived back at her turret flat after what had proved to be a rather long and exhausting day, she was for a few minutes almost too tired to take an interest in what to wear for the evening. She sank into a chair just inside the door to recover from the effort of walking upstairs, and looked down anxiously to see how her left ankle was bearing up. All she needed now, she thought, for her evening out with the handsome director was a hideously puffy ankle. But it seemed fine beneath the neat figure-of-eight support bandage that she'd worn all day, and which she intended to leave off for the evening, that was if she had the energy to go out at all, she thought somewhat morosely, feeling quite drained.

The telephone on her writing bureau started to ring, and she dragged her tired body from the chair to answer it. As she lifted the receiver, Gregory's voice said into her ear. 'And how did your first day back in harness go?'

'Oh,' she said, before recovering herself and subduing her thundering heartbeats at the unexpected sound of his voice. Energy began to flood back into her with the pleasure of hearing from him. 'Fine, just fine, thank you. I'm a bit tired, but nothing more, I'll be ready on time.'

'Don't worry about being on time; our table at the

restaurant will wait. The owner is by way of being a friend of mine. There's no hassle. I suggest that you sit down and drink a nice, ice-cold dry martini cocktail before you start rushing round getting ready. I'm sure you can do with a boost. Will you do that?'

'Oh, well, perhaps,' she mumbled. She felt stupid and unable to think of anything else to say; she was still trying to get over the fact that he was at the other end of the phone and had aptly guessed that she would be feeling half dead. What a surprising man he was, and so perceptive, to phone now as if he had known that she needed a bit of a lift.

'Is that a yes or a no? Perhaps I'd better pop over and mix you a drink myself; you sound quite helpless.' His voice held a hint of laughter, of intimacy that made her tummy churn with pleasure. He was teasing her in the nicest possible way.

'Oh, no, that won't be necessary, thank you. I can cope.' She gave a carefree laugh to hide the intense pleasure she felt at hearing from him at this opportune moment. Surely he must feel strongly about her to have bothered to enquire how she felt at the end of his own busy day, especially as he was seeing her later. She wasn't sure how he would explain his call, but curiosity made her ask, trying to sound casual, 'Gregory, what on earth made you ring now?'

There was a pause at the other end of the line, and then he said evenly, in almost impersonal tones, 'Well, you are a patient of mine, quite apart from being a valued colleague. I wanted to make sure that you weren't overdoing things on your first day back at work, as well as confirming that you are fit for this evening.' He made his reason sound very clinical.

She was disappointed; she had expected to hear him

say something warmer, more intimate. Well, that was her own fault; she shouldn't have asked such a leading question. 'I see,' she said brightly. 'Well, I haven't overdone it, and I'm looking forward to getting into full swing next week, and to going out tonight.'

'Splendid. Then I'll collect you at about half-past seven, but don't rush, and Erica. . .?'

'Yes?'

'Don't forget the dry martini; it's a great pick-me-up, and I want you to enjoy this evening.'

'I won't, and thank you, it was nice of you to call.'

'My pleasure.'

In spite of his cool tones towards the end, Gregory's call quite restored her flagging spirits. It gave her a warm feeling to know that he had been thinking of her, whatever reasons he gave for phoning. She prepared a drink as he had suggested, and sipped it while she considered what to wear. She eventually chose a nearly new, long, black-ribbed wool tunic top that clung to every curve, and at the same time emphasised her slenderness. It had a scooped-out, jewel-embroidered neckline, and she wore it over slim-fitting black velvet leggings, together with a pair of low-heeled black strappy sandals. She hooked on a pair of jade drop earrings that matched her eyeshadow, and brought out the emerald in her eyes as well as complementing the jewel embroidery of her tunic. Finally, she sprayed herself lavishly with her favourite perfume, and was ready. Sophisticated but casual, just right for a country club or an upmarket hotel, she decided, as she gave a final brush to the fringe of her gleaming mahogany hair.

The spring evening was fine and the sun just beginning to set when Gregory collected her at seven-thirty.

The sky was a mixture of purples and soft reds over the
downs to the west, and fluffy white clouds iridescent
with reflected colours above. It was a gorgeous evening, a perfect evening for her first outing in a month.
She was looking forward to it immensely.

'My dear, you look stunning,' Gregory said as Erica
opened the door of her flat. 'Absolutely right for where
we're dining, but then I'm sure you have all the right
instincts about these things: intelligence, beauty and
perception, the perfect combination.' He was half
teasing, half in earnest as, one well marked eyebrow
raised quizzically, he examined her from top to toe.

Erica gave him a dimpling smile. 'Thank you, sir.'
She bobbed a little curtsy. 'You look pretty good
yourself,' she said easily, admiring his formal black
evening jacket tailored to accommodate his wide
shoulders, and the neat bow-tie at the collar of his
plain white shirt. 'Very man-about-townish.'

'I blush at such compliments,' he said with an
unselfconscious chuckle, and no hint of a blush.
'Especially coming from a lovely lady like you.'

They were play-acting. Erica laughed softly. He bent
over her, and for a moment she thought that he was
going to kiss her on the mouth, but he didn't. He raised
her hand to his lips and kissed her fingers. Her hand
and heart trembled.

'Very Continental,' she said with commendable cool.

'My grandmother is French,' he said softly. 'Perhaps
that accounts for it.'

'Perhaps,' she murmured, laughing up at him.

'You'll need a wrap of some sort,' he said, his eyes
dark, serious. 'It'll be chilly later.'

'I have this,' she said, handing him a rainbow pastel-
coloured cashmere stole.

He placed it carefully, almost reverently, round her shoulders. 'Ready?' he asked, his face close to hers as he stood behind her.

She could feel his breath on her cheek, and smell his cologne mingling with his masculine smell. She felt weak, boneless, and had to resist the temptation to lean against him as his hands touched her shoulders.

'Ready,' she whispered, wondering as she did so what was happening to her. This man had the power to make her feel helpless and dependent, as well as admired. He was quite different from the stubborn, square-jawed man who sometimes irritated her, and with whom she always seemed to be arguing on matters involving his beloved Princes.

He operated on several levels, it seemed. He was the tough professional, ambitious negotiator in committee, unyielding, unwilling to give an inch except on his own terms, uncaring about making enemies if the need arose, aggressive, almost rude. Yet, as a doctor, he was gentle, caring, compassionate. And as a man? She thought that she had begun to get to know him on the several occasions they had met as friends, rather than as colleagues or doctor and patient. They had discovered much in common: a liking for similar music, paintings, books. Yet did she know him? There was the Scottish business, for instance. He hadn't properly explained that, though he had pretended to; he had in fact been distant and enigmatic and dismissive.

And tonight. . . tonight he was a different man yet again. There was nothing remote about him. His hands had lingered on her shoulders, and he had slightly tightened his hand on her left shoulder, though he had refrained from doing so on her injured right side. His breathing for a moment had been ragged and uneven,

and there was a softness, a tenderness, lurking in the
dark depths of his eyes, which she'd not seen before.
These thoughts raced through her mind as she looked
up and smiled at him.

He cleared his throat. 'Come,' he said huskily, as he
took her arm and guided her out of her flat and down
the wide staircase to the hall below. 'I've been waiting
for this evening for what seems a very long time.' He
sounded suddenly deadly serious; all banter had gone
from his voice and manner.

'I thought we were going to discuss our professional
differences,' she said demurely, as she looked up into
his now rather stern face, her heart in her mouth as he
grasped her arm more firmly.

To her amazement he said rather grimly. 'So did I,
but I fancy we have more personal matters to discuss,
don't you, Erica? You're a sophisticated woman; you
must know the effect that you're having on me,' His
incredibly dark eyes bored into hers as he looked
sideways down at her.

They had reached the front door. Slowly Gregory
turned her to face him fully, and then dropped his
hands to waist-level and linked his fingers behind her
back, drawing her close to him. She felt her breath
coming in short, uneven gasps. The hall was empty,
quiet, except for the crackling logs in the huge fireplace. The heady perfume from the many bowls of
spring flowers mingled with the scent of wood smoke
from the fire. Everything glowed in the firelight.

Whatever happens, I shall remember this moment
forever, thought Erica, as he lowered his face to meet
hers, and their lips touched. His lips met hers firmly at
first, and then they parted, and the tip of his tongue
teased about her lips until he prised them apart and

she let him invade her mouth with strong, thrusting intensity. She put up a hand, and ran her fingers through the silver border of hair at his temples. Even that, she thought, was strong, wiry and masculine. She felt herself responding to his thrusting tongue, using her own tongue in reply to his. They clung together in the silence as he kept her welded to him with his hands flat on the small of her back. She was aware of his male hardness, and welcomed it without any sense of repugnance or reserve. She was glad that he wanted her physically, as she realised that she wanted him in a way that she had never wanted any man before. This was no passing fancy; this was the real thing. This, for her at last, was love, true love. She gloried in being held to him, feeling the thrust of him, knowing that in this moment in time he wanted her with an almost explosive, pent-up passion.

At that moment, somehwere deep in her mind, she acknowledged that she loved and was in love with Gregory Hurst, for better or worse, whatever he felt for her. To him, perhaps, she was just a temporary temptation that might be physically satisfied. He was wedded to his work, as she had been wedded to hers. Neither of them had had time for a personal commitment. They were both confirmed to a single way of life, and at most might indulge in an affair, fleeting, passing, whatever stronger feelings might be involved. They were too late for loving. As the reality of the thought washed over her, Gregory, perhaps sensing her feelings, eased his mouth and body from hers, and stood her a little away from him. She was shaking from the intensity of what had passed between them, but, apart from a little uneven breathing, Gregory seemed much his usual self and totally in control.

Erica envied him. She wished that she might emulate his cool, but the feel of his body against hers, the way she had allowed him to kiss her, made her feel totally helpless. She didn't want to have to make decisions. She must leave it to him.

He smiled down at her. 'Erica,' he said softly, 'that was wonderful, thank you. But this is neither the time nor the place to bewitch each other. As I said earlier, we need to talk.' He opened the hall door, and pushed her gently out in front of him. 'We must try to be civilised about this, however difficult that is, don't you agree?'

Mutely she nodded. Words for the moment were beyond her. What did he mean by 'civilised'? Forget what had happened? Write it off as an interesting, sophisticated experience? Well, he might be able to do that, but she doubted that she could. His kiss and her response had meant too much to her. It had completely turned her world on its head. Even Patrick at his most loving, most amorous, hadn't been able to do that to her, and he had been pretty fervent at times.

For the first few minutes they drove in a pregnant, electric silence through the peaceful countryside, with the dusk descending about them. Erica stole a look sideways at Gregory as he drove with sure precision along the high-hedged, winding lanes. He was looking straight in front of him, apparently concentrating on the road ahead, but he must have been conscious of her look, for he turned and gave her a fleeting, reassuring smile, and patted her small hand with his large one. After a while they made occasional comments about the beauty of the pads of primroses that lined the banks, and remarked on the tender sprouting green leaves of the hedgerows, but otherwise they were silent. Erica was turning over and over in her mind what had just happened between herself and Gregory, and wondering if he had been as affected as she. Surreptitiously, she studied his stern profile as he drove, but could make nothing of it; he looked as calm and unmoved as ever.

The beauty of the sunset faded and the dark night sky took over, studded with stars. They turned down a lane that took them on to a road by the river, where houseboats and small sailing craft were anchored. After a short drive taking them to the estuary of the river, Gregory turned off on to a wooden quay.

'We have arrived,' he said, pointing to two large boats, linked together and festooned with fairy-lights, moored near the shore. 'The Anchorage — apt but rather unimaginative. But I assure you, it's only the name that's plebeian; the food and service are superb.'

Still recovering from the emotional upheaval that had occurred since Gregory had collected her from her flat, Erica pulled herself together, and said with forced cheerfulness, 'How lovely, it really looks a super place. It must be very popular.'

'It's beginning to build a reputation for itself with an elite clientele. People drive down from town to dine here; one normally has to book weeks ahead.'

'How did you discover it, and how on earth were you able to get a table at short notice?'

'The owner is a grateful patient; he will always find me a table.'

'Oh, I see — very useful, grateful patients.'

'Very,' replied Gregory drily.

He took her arm as she got out of the car, and she was glad of his support. It wasn't so much that her unstrapped ankle was paining her as that she felt in need of his touch.

They made their way across the canopied gangplank over a few feet of water, and stepped on to the deck of the boat. Here they were directed, by the waterside equivalent of a doorman, below decks to the restaurant, where a bearded, nautical-type figure came to meet them.

'Dr Hurst, good to see you,' boomed the bearded gentleman. 'And especially as you're escorting a lovely lady.' He bowed to Erica, and Gregory introduced them before their host led them to a secluded table, beneath a wide picture window that looked out over the river. Water slapped against the side of the boat with a faint phut phut, and there was the merest suggestion of movement on the lower deck. The dining-room might have been in any luxury restuarant; it was long, low and discreetly lighted by softly shaded lamps over each table.

A waiter appeared with menus in his hand, but Gregory waved the menus away. 'Will you accept what I suggest?' he asked Erica.

She nodded, not caring whether she ate or not. She just wished that they had gone somewhere quiet and private where they could have talked, and perhaps carried on from where their exhilarating kiss had left off. A wave of sensual pleasure swept over her as she recalled that kiss, and her toes curled at the memory of his hard body against hers, and all that it promised.

For a few moments she was conscious that her respirations were coming in short, shallow breaths, as if she had been running fast. She clenched her hands beneath the table, and looked across at Gregory, wondering if he felt as she did. His eyes met hers for a moment, and understanding flared in them, as if yet again he knew what she was thinking. He gave her a lop-sided smile and turned his attention to the waiter.

'We'll have the fish platter for starters,' he said, 'and baked trout with almonds to follow, with all the usual vegetables. And for pudding, Sussex Well.' He turned to Erica with a grin. 'About a thousand calories per mouthful, but worth a few furred-up arteries. Until you've tasted a Sussex Well, you haven't lived. It's a speciality here.'

His unspoken understanding, infectious good humour and the atmosphere of the Anchorage began to work its magic on her. She began to relax.

'It sounds wonderful,' she said. 'I believe that I'm going to enjoy it. I'm starving.'

She suddenly realised that this was true. In spite of all that had happened between herself and Gregory, she was ravenously hungry, having eaten just a sandwich for lunch after working hard all day. It didn't seem right, somehow, to be madly in love and yet hungry, but it was a fact.

'Good, I'm glad that you're not one of those females in nineteenth-century literature who fade away with unrequited love,' said Gregory with a grin. He stretched his hand across the table and touched her clasped fingers. She made to pull her hands away. 'Don't,' he said firmly, capturing them. 'Your love isn't unrequited — far from it.'

Her heart turned over. He seemed to be saying that he loved her. It was hard to believe, but could it be true? Was that long, passionate kiss a forerunner of the real thing?

'What do you mean?' she asked rather tremulously, her eyes wide, questioning. She felt like an innocent

girl rather than a mature woman, and certainly no
match for the strong, arrogant man opposite.

Gregory placed a long forefinger beneath her chin
and tilted her head back. She shivered at his touch.
'Those wonderful great green orbs,' he said softly. 'I
could drown in them. You have the most beautiful eyes
in the world, Miss Lang, do you know that?' He
removed his finger from her chin, and traced it across
her high cheekbones. 'You're so lovely, Erica. Your
bone-structure is perfect, your complexion flawless;
you leave me quite breathless with admiration.'

His words were wonderful to hear, but slowly Erica
regained her poise. She had heard such compliments
about her superb good looks before, and knew how to
deal with them. What she wanted to hear from this
man was more about love and sensitivity and intelligence, less about her superficial perfections. Her good
sense came to her rescue, and her years of resisting
male flattery. It was up to her to slow matters down.
Gregory would have to prove that he was not in the
same mould as other men if they were to further their
relationship.

'Such empty flattery,' she said with a laugh, 'will get
you nowhere.' She was being deliberately flirtatious.

Gregory gave a wry smile. 'I never supposed that it
would,' he said simply. 'But what I said came naturally
and from the heart.' For a moment he looked quite
grim. 'I don't doubt that you've heard similar things
said many times before, but I can assure you that my
sentiments are genuine.'

'Really?' Erica couldn't help sounding doubtful; it
was the sort of thing that he would say. He was a man
of the world, used to escorting beautiful women, and
he knew all the jargon. The long, seemingly sincere

kiss might be just part of his act. After all, someone as handsome as he, who had managed to stay a bachelor for so long, must have a talent for flattery. And that, she was suddenly convinced, was all it was. He had nothing more solid to offer; he was obviously looking for a brief, cheap affair with someone whom he found physically attractive who he thought could be easily hoodwinked. Well, that wasn't on her agenda. She loved him, whatever his feelings were for her, and unless he played the game her way she wasn't interested.

'Really,' he said, his eyes holding hers. 'I wouldn't deceive you, Erica.' He sounded totally sincere.

But then he would, she thought, her heart thumping painfully. She wanted so much to believe him, but experience had taught her that her particular brand of beauty attracted admiration from many sources. At best many admirers were weak and willing to be seduced by her beauty. At worst they wanted to prove that they could break down the barriers that she had erected over the years, and persuade her into a relationship. They had been easy to manipulate. She had never been in love with any of them. This time it was different. She was in love with Gregory, and she longed for him to be in love with her, not just for her beauty, but for her mind and heart. Only time, she thought, would prove whether that was true.

She said evenly 'Give me time, Gregory; I need time. We've only known each other a few weeks.' She looked at him imploringly. 'If you care enough, you will give me time.'

Gregory sat back in his chair, a wine glass between his fingers, and surveyed her beneath lowered lids. 'My dear girl,' he said quietly, reassuringly, 'I have no intention of rushing you.' His fascinating lop-sided grin appeared. 'I rather think that we have both been surprised by this evening's events, but I have no more intention of being overwhelmed by them than you have. We have all the time in the world to argue our way through this problem, as we have to date argued our way through others. I'm in no hurry to upset the status quo. I'm perfectly willing to enter into a long, slow—to use an old-fashioned world—courtship. In fact, it could be quite amusing. I won't rush you; I am, thank God, no longer a hot-blooded youth unable to contain myself.' There was a gleam in the depths of his dark eyes. 'Victory will be all the sweeter if waited for.'

Perversely, considering that it was she who had begged for time, Erica wished that he was not so willing to wait for matters to resolve themselves, especially in such an easy fashion. It was almost as if he was looking on it as a game. She felt indignant for a moment—not hot-blooded indeed! That wasn't the impression that he'd given when he'd kissed her. His passion had been only too obvious. Of course, the trouble was that he had too much self-control; he was too damned sure of himself. Part of her would have liked him to sweep her off her feet, and insist on making love to her without delay or care for her feelings; she almost regretted his sweet reasonableness. He couldn't possibly love her as she loved him if he was prepared to be so patient. She knew that she was being contrary, but couldn't help her wayward thoughts.

She bent her head lower over her plate, and looked at him through her long lashes. He was watching her, still with that knowing half-smile playing about his firm, sensual mouth, as if he read her thoughts. She lifted her head sharply, and looked him in the ey1. No man, not even the charismatic Gregory Hurst, whom she loved, was going to dictate to her. Victory, indeed. Well, victory would be hers, or at least shared, not his to boast about. She mustered all her calm and courage.

'How right you are,' she said with a sweet smile. 'Patience is perhaps a virtue that we don't value enough. Let us give ourselves time and space. I like the idea of your old-fashioned courtship. Let's put it into practice.'

'Let's,' said Gregory seriously, looking at her across the width of the table. 'We're both old enough and wise enough to appreciate the nuances.' He leaned forward and topped up her glass of wine, and when she picked it up he clinked his glass against hers. 'To us,' he said, 'and a leisurely old-fashioned courtship.'

'To us,' Erica heard herself saying, 'and an old-fashioned courtship.'

For the rest of the delicious meal they talked of many things as Gregory skilfully led the conversation away from themselves and to general matters that interested them both. At first Erica found it hard to turn her mind away from their intimate problems, but after a while she relaxed and began to enjoy herself. Just being with him was pleasure enough, and the thought of spending many more occasions in his company while they conducted their 'courtship' added a tantalising spiciness of anticipation to their growing relationship. She had no doubt that having Gregory court her in his own inimitable fashion would be a wonderful experience. He would be a superb lover, and their combined victory when — if? — they decided to commit themselves well worth waiting for.

CHAPTER TEN

By the time they left the Anchorage a large moon had arisen, bathing the landscape in a golden glow.

'If it weren't the wrong time of the year,' said Gregory, as they climbed into the Range Rover, 'I would say that it was a harvest moon.'

'At this time of year isn't it called a lovers' moon?' replied Erica, giving him a teasing smile.

'Ah, we're just right, then, for a smooch in the moonlight,' he laughed throatily. 'How very Victorian, an apt beginning to our formal courtship,' he teased back as he leaned across and fastened her seatbelt for her, brushing against her lightly as he did so. His eyes glittered in the moonlight and Erica shivered with pleasure at his touch. She pulled her stole closer round her shoulders.

'You're cold, I'll put the heater on,' he said as they pulled out of the restaurant car park.

'Thank you.'

They had not driven far along a narrow road between high hedges, making desultory conversation, when Gregory broke off what he was saying, and exclaimed, 'I believe there's a fire in those woods over there. Look, do you see? There's a hell of a lot of smoke hanging about it.' He pointed to a little copse of trees just ahead and to the right of them. Against the bright moonlit sky the smoky pall was clearly visible.

'Yes. Perhaps it's a barn or something on fire. Surely

154

it could hardly be the wood itself at this time of year? It's not dry as it is in the summer.'

'I think we'd better investigate.' He turned sharply into a narrow lane that bordered the wood straddling the hill. They came to a sharp bend, and the acrid smell of smoke was all about them, and they could hear the crackling, explosive noise of fire. They turned the corner.

A frightening sight met their eyes. A small cottage nestling among the trees was ablaze. Long tongues of flame and thick smoke crept up walls and billowed from broken windows on the ground floor, and silhou-etted against an eerie, smoky red background at a first-floor window was a woman with something in her arms.

'God,' said Gregory, as he pulled up with a jerk. 'She's got a baby.' He leapt out of the car while Erica was still undoing her seatbelt. 'Phone the fire brigade,' he shouted as he ran towards the cottage.

Automatically doing as he had instructed, almost paralysed with shock, Erica fumbled for the phone in the glove compartment, and as she did so saw the woman drop the bundle that she was holding into Gregory's outstretched arms, and then disappear.

She got through to the fire brigade and tried to speak calmly as she explained as best she could where they were. She gave the road number, and described the turning off it, and then asked for an ambulance to be sent as well as a fire engine. The minute she had finished phoning, she was out of the car, and at Gregory's side.

He handed her the baby and said grimly, 'This one seems all right, but there are two other children up there; the woman's gone for them. They must be in the room behind this one. I'll have to stay here to catch

them; they'll be too heavy for you. We could use a
ladder so that I could get up there. See if you can find
one when you've seen to the baby.'

Erica nodded as she took the baby, bundled in a cot
blanket, to the car, and laid it carefully on the back
seat. It was grizzling quietly, but seemed unhurt and
unaffected by smoke, and breathed quite naturally.

As she turned back towards the cottage, the woman
appeared again in the window, clutching a small child
in each arm. 'Catch them,' she shrieked, and heaved
one child over the ledge. Gregory moved in time to
catch him, but the falling weight of the child almost
took him off balance. Erica rushed forward and helped
him steady himself, and then took the child from him.
He moved back beneath the window as a huge puff of
smoke, followed by a tongue of fire, lit up the room
behind the woman. The fire was escalating fast.

'Jump, both of you,' he shouted. 'I'll break your
fall.'

Erica dumped the first child on the grass and stood
beside him. Without taking his eyes off the woman,
Gregory said tersely, 'Get the car rug.' Erica raced
back to the car.

She heard Gregory call again to throw the child
down, but the woman seemed frozen, unable to jump,
unable to release the third child from her arms.

Breathless, Erica returned with the rug. 'Save the
child,' she called urgently. 'We've got a rug.' She and
Gregory held the rug out between them a few feet from
the ground.

The woman gave an inarticulate cry, and hurled the
small figure out of the window, then she dropped out
of sight below the window-ledge. They caught the small
but fairly weighty body in the rug, which miraculously

didn't tear, and lowered him to the ground. He was coughing and tears were trickling down his smoke-grimed face, but he seemed to be breathing without too much difficulty.

Erica lifted the boy up. He was perhaps four years old and quite heavy. She held him against her shoulder, patting his back as she did so. 'Cough it up, love, and take nice deep breaths,' she said softly as she hurried back with him to the car. She propped him up in the corner beside the baby, held her handkerchief to his nose, and told him to blow. He did so, feebly at first, and then more vigorously. When she was sure that he was reasonably comfortable, she returned for the other, younger boy, who was still sitting silently where she had left him on the grass.

'I've got to get up there,' Gregory said. 'I'm going round the back; the stairs might be passable. She's fainted or succumbed to the smoke and heat. You check the children for respiratory inhalation damage and get an ambulance.

'It's on the way, with the fire brigade, and the children don't seem too bad.'

'Right.' He nodded and disappeared at a run round the side of the house.

Erica briefly examined the three children in the car. The oldest child had stopped coughing, and his nose now seemed pretty clear, though his eyes were still watering. Like his younger brother, who was sitting with his thumb in his mouth, he seemed more dazed and shocked than anything, though he did ask pathetically for 'Mummy' as Erica covered him and his brother with her stole.

'She'll be here soon,' Erica promised, praying that it would be true. 'You be a good boy, and look after your brother and the baby. I'm just going to get Mummy now.'

She returned to stand beneath the window in case the woman appeared again and decided to try to jump. What she would do if this happened, she hadn't a clue. If Gregory was back, they might try to break her fall with the rug, though it had only just held for the child when he'd dropped into it; it was unlikely that it would take the weight of an adult. Still, it might help.

She clenched her fists to stop her hands trembling as she wondered what was happening to Gregory. Was he trying to fight his way through the burning building? Was he in danger? Her heart turned over at the thought, and a great wave of sickness swept over her. Please, God, let him be all right, she prayed.

At that moment he came round the corner of the cottage carrying a ladder. Erica closed her eyes for a moment in sheer relief at the sight of him, before going forward to help him with the ladder.

'Stairs are well alight,' he said tersely. 'Can't get up that way.' He leaned the ladder against the wall. It reached to just beneath the window. 'Steady the bottom,' he added as he started up the first few rungs. 'I might have to bring her down with me if she can't make it on her own.'

'Right.' She wanted to say all sorts of things about taking care, but there wasn't the time. All she could do was to steady the ladder, and hope that the woman was conscious enough to help herself. He climbed the ladder and disappeared through the window into the burning room.

The next few moments seemed endless before he re-appeared at the window. 'She's semi-conscious,' he called down. 'I'm going to carry her down. Hang on to this bloody thing.' He turned his back to the window and she could see the woman slung across his shoulders. He put one leg over the low sill, feeling with his toe for a rung in the ladder. He found it and brought his other foot over the sill, ducking as he did so with his burden to clear the top of the window. For a moment his head and the hump of the woman across his shoulders were silhouetted against the fiery backdrop of the room, then he cleared the window and started his journey downwards.

The ladder shook ominously and Erica hung on to it for dear life, trying to keep it steady, as slowly and carefully he made his way down rung by rung.

At that moment the sound of a fire engine approaching a long way off broke through the noise of the crackling fire.

Erica could almost have wept with relief. 'Thank God,' she muttered as she clung to the foot of the ladder.

Gregory, with the woman suspended round his neck and shoulders, made his way to the ground. Gently he released her from his grasp and with Erica's help lowered her on to the grass. Her eyes flickered open and she coughed a little.

That's good,' said Gregory hoarsely as he cleared his own throat. 'Cough again.' He supported her with one hand, and gently pummelled her back with his other hand.

She coughed and spluttered. 'My children?' she gasped. 'Are they hurt?'

'No, they're fine,' said Erica firmly. 'I'm a nurse and I've made them comfortable in the car. Don't worry about them; they are quite safe. And this gentleman's a doctor — Dr Hurst. He'll check them in a moment, and the ambulance will be here soon. But we're more concerned about you; you must have inhaled a lot of smoke.'

'Not too much. I kept going to the window. I'm all right. I just fainted, I think. I'm not burnt or anything, but I must see my children, I must.'

'Yes, of course,' said Gregory calmly. 'You'll see them right now. Do you think you can manage to walk with our help?'

'Oh, yes. Just let me get to my children.'

Together Erica and Gregory supported the woman across to the Range Rover. 'The baby's asleep,' explained Erica, 'and the other two are shocked but otherwise all right.'

At the sight of their mother, the boys started to cry, and the baby woke up and started to grizzle. The young mother tried to hug and reassure them all, and hold back her own tears.

Briefly Gregory checked the family over and confirmed that they were all breathing normally, and were as comfortable as it was possible to make them in the circumstances. He took off his dress jacket and draped it round the woman's shoulders to give her extra warmth. There was really nothing else that he and Erica could do now that the family were safe and the fire brigade and ambulance were on their way.

They were leaning against the Range Rover, recovering from their efforts, when the first fire engine arrived, closely followed by an ambulance. It was with overwhelming relief that, after a few minutes' conversation with the chief fire officer and the paramedic, they handed over to these experts.

Very quickly mother and children—the Lomax family, as they then learned their name to be—were transferred from the car to the ambulance. A tearful Mrs Lomax thanked them for rescuing her and her children, before being driven away to the local hospital.

At last Erica and Gregory were free to leave.

But they couldn't tear themselves away from the burning cottage at once, and they stood propped against the car, watching the fireman at work, grimly playing their powerful hoses on the blaze. Against the night sky, even lit as it was by moonlight, flames and sparks flashed ominously, seeming to lick at the tops of the nearby trees. They had a few more words with the senior fire officer, who told them that he thought that the fire was coming under control, though there would be little of the building left.

He didn't yet know what had caused it; Mrs Lomax didn't smoke, and hadn't been cooking late. 'Probably faulty wiring,' he said. 'But at least there were no deaths or serious injuries in this fire, which makes a change.'

He returned to his men, and Erica and Gregory prepared to leave.

Now that the adrenalin caused by the emergency was beginning to subside, and after her already busy working day, Erica was feeling exhausted. She looked sideways at Gregory, still leaning against the Range Rover, and saw that he was similarly affected. He was looking drawn beneath his smoke-smeared face — not surprising, after his efforts at rescuing the children and their mother. He had been adamant that he hadn't been affected by the smoke, but she was beginning to wonder if he should have gone to hospital for a check-up, or had a whiff or so of oxygen before the ambulance left. And she should have insisted on him having some treatment — not of course that he would have taken any notice; he was too concerned about Mrs Lomax and the children.

Well, she could help a little; she could at least save him the effort of driving back to Princes. 'I'll drive,' she said firmly, managing a tired smile, and added in a teasing voice which she hoped would make him more amenable to her suggestion, 'You need a rest after all those heroics, my dear doctor. You should really have gone to the local hospital for a check-up.'

Gregory looked down at her, smiled wryly, and shook his head. 'You're pretty done in yourself,' he said. 'And no way, my dear girl, am I going to allow you to drive; you're still recovering from two gammy legs, remember? You've been using a stick until this evening. And be assured, I'm, fine.' He thumped his chest and wheezed a bit, and pulled a face. 'Well, almost, and I promise I will get our own casualty people to check me over when we get back to Princes, if necessary.'

She hesitated before getting into the passenger seat, and Gregory gave her a push. 'I mean it, Erica,' he said with quiet authority. 'I'm driving, no argument.'

With a shrug, Erica climbed into the vehicle, and Gregory walked round to the driver's seat and climbed in, switched on the engine, and started off. 'Good girl,' he said softly, and patted her hand.

'Don't patronise me,' she said fiercely, the conflicting emotions of the evening fuelling her irritation. Impatiently she pulled her hand away from beneath his, though she knew that he was right about her not yet being fit to drive. 'I'm only doing this because it makes sense, not because you want to prove that you're macho enough to drive after all that has happened.' Suddenly she felt quite tearful, presumably because of the stresses of the last couple of hours, and her concern for the Lomax family, and the fright she had had when Gregory was in the burning building.

The reality of what had happened seemed to make a nonsense of their carefree evening and talk of a long, slow courtship. What rubbish. Why had she asked for time before committing herself to the love that she felt for Gregory. What did it matter that he might not be in love with her as she was with him? What if he had been killed or injured in the fire? She might have lost him without ever having made love to him. It was all pride, but what did pride matter in the face of near death? Tonight's incident brought everything into focus. It was a reminder that she should make the most of every day, especially where love was concerned. To wait to express her love was foolish. Be honest, tell him how you feel, all her instincts cried out.

They had driven some miles in silence, both tired and wrapped in their thoughts. Erica wanted to break the silence, but didn't know how; she only knew that she must tell Gregory how she now felt. It was the only honest thing to do. She had wanted time to come to terms with her feelings for him, but, though he had agreed, his kiss at the beginning of the evening had told her that he was ready for a physical relationship now. Well, after the events of this evening, so was she. She would play it his way, and, as for the Scottish business, she would accept his explanation without question until he further enlightened her. And she would tell him the truth about Larry, and not pretend any more that there was anything between her and him.

She knew, after the events of the evening, that the time had come for being honest with each other. It seemed simple, but how to go about doing so? Should she just pour out her feelings, and hope that he would do likewise, or should she give herself a day or two to come to terms with those feelings?

She glanced at Gregory's tired but still stern profile, dimly seen in the moonlight, and knew that he would know what to do. She could leave all the decisions to him, and, for once in her well ordered and responsible life, be pleased to do so. With a sudden overwhelming sense of relief, she gave a great sigh and turned towards Gregory. Simultaneously, he took his eyes from the road for a moment and glanced at her, and as she said, 'Gregory,' he said,

'Erica.'

They both laughed as they broke the brooding silence, and released the tension.

'You first,' said Gregory, giving her a lovely smile.

'No, you,' said Erica, suddenly shy, and wanting to know what he had to say.

'I was thinking about the Lomaxes, and how an accident has changed their lives in a few hours.'

'Oh, the Lomaxes.' Disappointment hit her; she had hoped that he might have had more personal thoughts.

'And it made me think about us, Erica, and whether we were right to talk about having all the time in the world. What happened this evening rather makes a nonsense of that line of thinking. We should know in our profession that life's too short to take chances with, to let pride or anything else stand in the way of love. Perhaps we needed an outside incident like this to jerk us to our senses.'

'Oh, Gregory.' This time she was too overwhelmed to say more, because his thoughts had been so exactly like hers. It was wonderful. 'Oh, Gregory,' she repeated breathlessly. 'That's exactly what I was thinking.'

He took a grimy hand off the steering-wheel and patted her knee. 'I rather imagined that we might be having parallel thoughts,' he said softly. 'You were radiating love and longing.'

'Was I?'

'Oh, yes. It was coming over to me powerfully, your thought waves.'

'I'm so glad you were receptive and didn't try to block me out.'

'I'd never block you out, Erica; you've had my ear since the first day we met, when dear old Mrs Howard went walkabout. Your lovely green eyes slayed me, then.'

'Really?'

'Really. I remember thinking, Such a beautiful woman, do hope she's not just passing through. And then a bit later I realised who you were, and my heart sank.'

'Why did it sink?'

'Because I'd vetoed your apppointment, and I knew that we were going to argue like mad over almost everything to do with work.'

'And you were right, and we have.'

'I know, and the fact that we feel the way we do about each other is not going to make the slightest difference in committee. I shall still argue with you, Erica, on issues like selling off land for development and letting our Princes' property to a bunch of charlatans.'

In spite of all that had happened, and all her good intentions, Erica's blood rose. 'But you promised you

wouldn't block me on that; you said that at least you
would let it go forward for discussion. You said——'

'I said that I would, and I will, but my darling,
beautiful, lovely Erica, I will fight you all the way.'

'And I, you,' she said fiercely. She felt the blood
beating in her cheeks, and her pulses racing. 'Just
because I love you won't make the slightest difference.'

'Of course it won't,' said Gregory, infuriatingly calm,
'and I wouldn't appreciate it if it did.' He grinned
broadly. 'Look,' he said, 'we're nearly home—at my
home, at the Small House. It's just off the road along
here before we get to the main gates. Come in and let
battle——' he paused suggestively '—or love com-
mence.' He gripped her knee. 'You don't want me to
take you back to your flat, do you?'

He pulled in on the gravel sweep of drive in front of
an elegant eighteenth-century house, and as soon as he
had stopped reached out a hand and placed it under
her chin, tilting her head till her eyes met his. 'Do you,
Erica?'

She shook her head. 'No,' she whispered. 'I don't.'

'Good.' He released her seatbelt, heaved himself out
of the car, and came round to assist her from the
passenger seat.

'I've been longing to see you in my own home,' he
said. 'Welcome to the Small House.' He slipped his
key into the lock, and opened the door.

Erica stepped into the narrow but elegant hall lit by
wall lamps. A graceful, shallow staircase, all rich blue
carpet and white paintwork, curved its way up to the
first floor.

'Oh, Gregory, it's charming, so cool, so——'

Gregory put an arm round her waist, and turned her

to face him. 'Like you,' he murmured. 'You're charming, and just as cool, just as ——'

'Gregory,' said a voice from above them. 'At last you're home. I thought that you would never come.'

Gregory, still holding Erica in his arms, glanced upwards. Eric followed his gaze.

A woman with a thick mane of red hair, and wearing a filmy négligé, stood silhouetted in the light at the top of the stairs.

'Good God, Helen!' exclaimed Gregory. 'What on earth is she doing here?'

They both stood as still as statues for a moment, Gregory with his hands linked round Erica's waist, as they stared at the figure standing at the top of the stairs.

Gregory's hands tightened around Erica. His face was grim and set. 'Stay here,' he said abruptly. 'I'll deal with her.'

Erica took hold of his wrists as he released his hands from behind her back. She was ice-cold, yet at the same time something seemed to be exploding inside her. 'Yes,' she said, in a fierce, thin voice. 'You deal with your Helen, but you take me home first, and if you won't take me I'll walk.' Her eyes, like flints, met his fathomless dark ones. She rushed on before he could speak. 'I don't want to know anything, hear anything about her, about anything. Oh, how could you? Just take me home. We're finished, Gregory, finished before we've even started.'

There was a lump inside her that was like a stone, and all she wanted to do was to get away from the figure at the top of the stairs — Helen, the Scottish connection. She could feel hysteria building up inside her. She had to leave before she gave way to inane laughter, or to tears.

Her head was pounding with a dozen jumbled thoughts as Gregory easily slipped his hands from her grasp and then held both of hers in his. In a firm, reasonable voice, he said with a calm that set her teeth on edge, 'Erica, I appreciate that you're shocked by Helen's appearance, but don't over-react. Of course I know that you want to go home now, and of course I'll drive you there, but I must have a moment to speak to Helen first. Some emergency has brought her all the way down from Scotland. Now please, don't rush away; I'll be with you, and I'll explain.'

He looked up to where Helen still stood, silently gazing down at them.

Erica pulled her hands from his and turned away from him. 'I won't wait,' she said icily, fear clutching at her heart. 'I insist that you take me home straight away, and then you can come back to your precious Helen and spend the rest of your life with her as far as I'm concerned.' She took a deep, shuddering breath and added, 'I'm just grateful to her for arriving before I'd made a complete fool of myself, and let you get me into your bed.' She dragged her eyes away from his.

'Don't be vulgar, Erica,' said Gregory in equally icy tones. 'It's just not you.'

'Vulgar?' she said with a hard laugh. 'You don't need lessons in vulgarity, Dr Hurst. You've reached rock-bottom, with promises to one woman and another waiting to hop into the sack with you.'

Gregory took her chin in one hand none too gently, forcing her to face him. 'I'll forgive you all this non-sense, Erica, because you're in shock and you're hysterical, but don't say another word, or you'll make me do something that I would rather not. Now just wait there till I'm ready to take you home. Don't move. I mean it, Erica, do — not — move.'

She had never seen his eyes so black, nor his face so grim, nor heard him speak with such authority. He turned his back on her and climbed the stairs three at a time. Erica stood for a moment, immobile, then turned and fled through the door.

She limped down the drive. Her ankle was throbbing painfully, but resolutely she made her way along the road towards the entrance to Princes.

She had only gone a short distance when the Range Rover pulled up beside her.

'Get in,' Gregory said harshly.

'Why should I?'

'Because you can't damn well walk up to the manor house.'

'I can.'

'My dear girl——'

'Don't you "dear girl" me. I'm not anyone's dear girl, and certainly not yours,' she spat out.

'Don't be so damned childish. Get in or I'll get out and drag you in.' His voice was hard with barely suppressed rage. His eyes glittered dangerously. She had never seen him so angry, so venomous. He was quite frightening.

She knew that he had meant all that he had said, and she knew too that she was incapable of walking up the mile-long drive. She limped over to the car and climbed in, huddling herself up into the corner near the door, as far as she could from Gregory.

Within a couple of minutes they were entering the drive to Princes Park, and it was then that Gregory spoke in a quiet and matter-of-fact voice.

'Erica, I'm sorry this happened, Helen turning up out of the blue. It couldn't be worse, especially after the sort of evening we've had, a mixture of magic and trauma. I'm not surprised you were thrown for a bit. I dare say we both said things we'd rather not have said; our behaviour certainly wasn't in character, was it?'

Erica wanted to agree with him, wanted to find a way of making her peace with him, but some perverse streak prevailed; she was so desperately hurt. 'I meant everything that I said,' she muttered through clenched teeth. 'I don't want anything more to do with you, Gregory, except professionally. I was right to be wary of you when we first met; I should have stayed that way, and not let you persuade me otherwise. I'm ashamed of myself for falling for that line of yours when I asked you about your Scottish commitment. Just a distant relative you were helping out. What rubbish.' Her voice got more shrill as she finished speaking, and tears of sadness, frustration and rage pricked her eyes. She turned her head away and stared unseeingly out at the night sky.

Gregory made an exasperated sound in his throat. 'For God's sake, don't get hysterical again,' he said sharply. 'I've had enough of hysterical, weepy women for one night.' He was silent for a bit, and then in more patient tones said, 'You have a right to feel affronted by what has happened, Erica, but don't over-estimate it; let me explain about Helen.'

'I don't want to hear about that woman.'

'It isn't what you think.'

'Ha, that's what all men say when they are trying to wriggle out of something unpleasant.' Her voice was disbelieving, contemptuous.

They pulled up in front of the Old House, and Erica began to unbuckle her seatbelt.

Gregory said in an arctic voice, 'I am not all men, Erica. I don't hide behind women's frailties, and neither do I expect to have to explain myself repeatedly. If and when you are ready to accept the truth about my "Scottish connection", tell me. Perhaps you were right in suggesting that we don't meet on a personal basis for the time being. I certainly won't force myself on you.'

He got out of the car, came round to the passenger side, and opened the door.

Swallowing her tears and unhappiness, Erica stepped down from the Range Rover, blindly accepting the hand that he courteously offered. He held his hand out for the key that all residents were given, and unlocked the massive front door. She turned and took it from him as he handed it back to her. Without meaning to, she let her eyes meet his. They were dark, but luminous, and in spite of his words his whole face bore an expression of compassion and understanding. More than anything in the world she wanted to throw herself into his strong arms, and beg his forgiveness.

Forgiveness for what! Pride came to her aid. 'Thank you,' she said, 'for seeing me home; I can manage now.' She stepped into the dimly lit hall, and closed the door.

Slowly, methodically, Erica made her way upstairs, where, zombie-like, she undressed, showered, and lay down on her bed. There she remained staring into the dark for the rest of the night.

CHAPTER ELEVEN

THE weekend passed for Erica with a terrible relentlessness. She felt hollow, restless and emotionally numb after the events of that Friday evening. She turned over and over in her mind what had happened. There had been Gregory's passionate kiss and embrace, and later his almost certain admission that he was in love with her, which had so warmed and thrilled and slightly scared her and had begun what promised to be a magical evening.

Then there had been their discussion over the delicious meal at the Anchorage, when Gregory had seemed to understand her reservations about falling in love, and had been patient and kind, and agreed to play a waiting game to please her. This had been wiped out later when they had experienced an even greater understanding following the fire, and they had been drawn together like magnets, making waiting seem nonsensical and love all that mattered.

And so it might have been, Erica told herself, if they had consummated their love that night. But the beautiful Helen had turned up. True, Gregory had been surprised; true, he had wanted to explain about her and she had not given him time. But it was ludicrous to believe what he had told her before; that Helen was just the widow of a relative whom he was helping. A woman like that, with sultry looks and a sultry voice, was made to charm an eligible bachelor like Gregory, and he must know it, and must have responded to it.

Try as she might, Erica couldn't believe what Gregory had implied; that there was nothing between him and Helen Hurst.

So her tortured thoughts swayed her one way and another. Several times over that weekend she almost called him, almost asked him to give his version of the situation, but something stopped her. It was cowardly, but at times she decided that she would rather live with uncertainty than perhaps have him reveal some unpalatable truth, or, worse, lie. Why doesn't he contact me? she thought, although she knew the answer. He had been willing to explain Helen's role in his life, but she hadn't wanted to know. He wasn't the sort of man to risk being rebuffed a second time.

She pictured his incredibly handsome face, his vigorous black hair with the distinguished touches of silver at his temples and his dark, fathomless eyes. She felt again the strength of his arms round her and his lean, muscled body against hers when he had kissed her with such passion. For a big, broad-shouldered man he could be physically gentle if he chose, but he could be hard and unyielding, like the granite of his native Scotland. He had moral strength too, and mental toughness. Well, she told herself belligerently, she too could be mentally tough, and he would have to wait a long time for her to go crawling to him and give him personal satisfaction.

Her belligerence and anger helped her maintain her distance. But though she held back over their personal affairs, she didn't pull any punches when it came to fighting issues in committee.

On the Monday following a desolate weekend, both Erica and Gregory spoke eloquently at the policy and resources meeting about the alternative-medicine issue.

Erica called attention to the fact that several of the best teaching hospitals were now doing trials involving alternative medicine in certain fields, and were hopeful of results.

Gregory remained scathing and sceptical and talked about giving people false hope. 'There may be the occasional response to some of these rather peculiar remedies,' he conceded scornfully, 'but I have witnessed personally the havoc that a so-called cure had on a friend and his family. Believing that he was improving raised their hopes, and made his dying harder to take.' His dark, intelligent gaze came to rest on Erica.

He means Helen's husband, she thought, her eyes meeting his, suddenly feeling wretched for not realising earlier that his antagonism towards alternative medicine might have been well founded. He had hinted as much.

He continued. 'And I am not alone; many of my medical colleagues agree that alternative or holistic medicine is at best useless, at worst distressing.' His eyes held hers. 'Perhaps,' he said softly, 'Miss Lang has been rather hasty in supporting this motion, and would like time to consider it further before pushing for a result in the near future.'

She knew that he was alluding to their personal situation as well as the professional one, and he was in a sense offering her a chance to let him know that she was willing to listen to him. Well, she wouldn't; she couldn't. Neither on the personal nor the professional front was she prepared to give in to him. It was up to him to prove his case, on both counts.

She tilted her chin up and looked him straight in the eye. In a sweet, mocking sort of voice, and giving him a delightful smile, she said, 'I must thank Dr Hurst for his suggestion that I not pursue this matter immediately, but I have in fact given it a great deal of thought over the last few weeks, and collected data of interest, copies of which you will find in front of you. Of course I am a newcomer to Princes. But I must also point out that I too have this hospital's good name at heart, and that it is my job to put forward other people's points of view as well as my own, and that is precisely what I am doing. I don't speak just on my own account, on this matter at least.'

Let him make what he wants to of that, she thought angrily as she lowered her eyes, and scribbled a meaningless note on the pad in front of her. But her heart was heavy as lead; she didn't want to be fighting with him on this or any other issue. If only he had been honest with her about his Scottish affair, had admitted it, but said that it was in the past, it would have been bearable; but to deny it, even when the woman turned up in his house in seductive attire, just didn't ring true.

With an effort, she reminded herself that she was working, and focused on what was happening round the committee table.

The chairman called for a vote on the issue, and by a small majority it was agreed to pursue the matter of renting out the Dower House to a number of well vetted and qualified practitioners of alternative, holistic and complementary medicine.

A decision on the sale of land to a property speculator was postponed yet again to the next meeting, while further facts were gathered.

Erica then put forward her proposal that the visitors' car parking facilities should be discussed, and was surprised and pleased to get Gregory's unequivocal support on this. She looked at him across the table, and received a sardonic grin from him. Whatever he felt, now that the voting was over, he was not going to be rattled by the committee's decision to consider the scheme for the Dower House, though clearly he would go on opposing it tooth and nail, but that of course was the strength of the man.

The meeting at last came to an end, and Erica hurried from the room, politely avoiding getting into conversation with anybody. All she wanted to do was to get back to her office, and from there, when she had finished her chores for the day, retire to her flat.

Her flat over the next few weeks became an oasis, a sanctuary. When not working, she spent much of her time there, reading, playing discs, enjoying—or perhaps, more accurately, enduring—her solitude. It wasn't that she was short of invitations to dine or take drinks with the many new friends that she had made at Princes; it was a case of not wanting to socialise. She was content at the moment with her own company, her own thoughts.

She went to supper with Clare Dunn a couple of times, almost succumbing to the temptation to confide in the older woman, tell of her mixed feelings relating to Gregory, knowing that she would have a sympathetic hearing. But she didn't. Neither could she bring herself to ask Clare for more information about Helen Hurst, or discuss with her that lady's presence in the Small House. Somehow it would have seemed like a betrayal of Gregory. Perhaps Clare felt the same, for she didn't volunteer any information either.

One afternoon Erica took tea with Lady Violet in her crumbling mansion on the outskirts of Princes

Hollow, and enjoyed her visit with that eccentric old lady. And on another occasion she accepted an invitation for dinner from Larry Grey, the head of the pain clinic, who wanted to thank her for what she had done on behalf of his unit, via her support for the alternative-medicine scheme. The evening was enjoyable, and Larry very attentive, but all the time she was imagining what it would have been like if she had dined with Gregory.

That was the trouble. Her thoughts these days, when she was not occupied at work, revolved round and round Gregory. She had heard on the grapevine that his visitor from Scotland had left after a few days, but nobody knew or said anything else about her. There seemed to be a conspiracy of silence about the beautiful Helen, and after a while Erica began to wonder uneasily if this was because there was nothing to say about her, nothing for the gossips to get their teeth into.

Slowly it began to dawn on her that maybe Gregory had been telling the truth when he'd said that there was nothing between him and the attractive widow. Perhaps there was a perfectly understandable explanation for her being in his house in the early hours of the morning, as he had implied. And maybe she was just wearing a flimsy négligé because she was accustomed to doing so. It was possible. Erica's thoughts raced on as she stared unseeingly down from the turret window at the beds of late spring flowers, where daffodils had given way to scarlet tulips and purple irises. Perhaps she had simply jumped to conclusions because she was. . . Go on, she said to herself, say it; you were jealous. After all, she knew nothing about the Scottish woman except what she had conjured up in her imagination, largely because Gregory had dismissed her so arbitrarily.

But supposing he had been arbitrary because it was exactly as he had said, and Helen was simply the widow of a relation who needed help with her affairs, and she meant no more than that to him? Erica felt her cheeks go hot and cold with embarrassment and shame. Supposing that was the truth? How could she have thought so badly of him? He might be unbearably arrogant at times, but he was honourable. He wouldn't stoop to deceiving her; it was incredible that she could ever have thought so.

Suddenly it all seemed so clear, as clear as the rain-washed sky arching over the parkland. Gregory hadn't deceived her, she had deceived herself, and she had done it to avoid committing herself to him, because she thought herself committed to work and past falling in love. She liked her ordered, responsible way of life, and had instinctively tried to protect it. But she was learning that love wouldn't be denied; these last few miserable weeks had proved that.

She sat motionless for a while, gazing at the delicate blue and gold of the spring evening, as she marshalled her thoughts. For the first time since that catastrophic Friday, her mind, though busy, was at peace. She had reached a decision. It wouldn't be easy, but she would have to confront Gregory, and tell him that she was ready to listen to whatever he had to say. She would sink her pride, and go to him.

When?

Why not now? she answered herself. She could phone him, and arrange to visit him this evening. Her heart thumped painfully at the thought of speaking directly to him on a personal basis for the first time in weeks. She had a momentary qualm as she reached for the phone. Supposing he no longer wanted to revive their fragile relationship? He had been casually polite whenever they had met recently, but there had been nothing in his manner to convey any deeper feelings. But, when they had parted so stormily that Friday night, he had intimated that he would always be ready to listen if she approached him, and he had meant it. With a surge of relief, she knew that he wouldn't have changed his mind.

She picked up the phone and dialled the Small House.

CHAPTER TWELVE

THE phone rang several times before it was answered, and Gregory's voice spoke in her ear.

'Good evening, Hurst speaking.'

Erica almost dropped the receiver at the sound of his brisk tone. He didn't sound any too pleased at having been interrupted in whatever he was doing.

She swallowed, and for a moment couldn't get any words out.

'Who is this?' asked Gregory even more impatiently.

She found a whisper of a voice. 'It's me, Erica. I'm sorry to disturb you.'

'Erica!' Surprise and not annoyance was in his voice now. 'Erica,' he repeated and cleared his throat. His voice sounded coolly friendly when he spoke again. 'What can I do for you?'

'I. . .I'm not sure; I want to talk.'

'Now?' he almost barked out.

'Y. . .yes, if it's convenient.'

'I'll make it bloody convenient,' he rasped out, 'though I'm up to my eyes in paperwork. Where do you want to meet?'

'I thought your place, the Small House,' she said uncertainly.

There was a pause before he replied with a hint of amusement in his voice, 'You're not afraid of ruining my reputation, then, visiting as dusk falls?'

He must be teasing. Her uncertainty diminished a fraction. 'I didn't know that you had a reputation to ruin,' she said with a small laugh. 'I thought it was rock-solid.'

'And so it is,' he said firmly. 'It is capable of withstanding a few slings and arrows, even aimed by the grapevine.'

So he had guessed that the gossips had been at work, and not discovered anything. He must know, too, that she had heard nothing of importance concerning Helen's visit. Had his particular brand of perception made it possible for him to divine what she wanted to say to him?

She said, with all the calm that she could muster, 'So may I call to see you, Gregory? It won't take me long to drive over.'

'Don't drive,' he said. 'Walk. Across the park. I'll meet you halfway. The dogs need an outing.'

'Dogs?' she asked stupidly.

'A brace of red setters—Bruce and Cissie. You would have met them on your last visit, had you stayed longer.'

Was there a hint of sarcasm?

'Oh.' She gathered the remnants of her pride about her. 'I look forward to meeting them this time,' she said. 'I have rather a penchant for red setters. I grew up with them.'

'Good, then you won't mind the odd muddy paw.'

'Not a bit.'

'I'll start out now; see you in, say, a quarter of an hour.'

'Fine.'

Gregory had been right about dusk falling, Erica realised as she left the Old House. The sky had turned purple, and the glorious rainbow colours of sunset had disappeared. The flowerbeds glowed subduedly in the half-light and the scent of the dark velvet wallflowers filled the near darkness.

She struck out eastwards across the park, following the line of the stately Spanish chestnuts in the direction of the Small House. She had been walking for several minutes when a pair of dogs came bounding up to her, a gorgeous pair of red setters.

She stooped to pat their silky heads, and then looked up. Gregory was standing a few feet from her, silently watching her greet the dogs.

'Gregory,' she said uncertainly, feeling at a loss, not knowing what else to say. She stared at him, drinking in his nearness, longing to be closer to him. He was wearing a pale, button-through blouson which emphasised his broad, bulky shoulders. His face, though she knew that it was lightly tanned, showed pale in the near darkness.

'Erica.' His voice sounded rich and deep. He ducked beneath a low branch of one of the chestnuts, and came towards her, holding out both hands. She put hers into his, and he grasped them firmly, warmly.

The dogs gambolled around them.

He drew her towards him, and she could feel, rather than see, his dark eyes boring into hers as she got closer.

They stood, body almost touching body, and stared at each other.

Erica spoke first, huskily, all the carefully prepared phrases flying out of her head. 'Gregory, I believe I've been an absolute fool.'

Even in the dim light, she could see his mouth quirk. 'Not a fool, my darling, never a fool,' he said softly. 'You're bright and clever, and I love you for it. But thank God you're female and have a modicum of jealousy where I'm concerned.

'Jealousy? A modicum?' she repeated.

'Because of Helen; because you thought that she represented competition, and you were afraid to listen to reason. That makes you female, and perceptive, and open to suggestion.'

Erica pushed herself away from him a little. 'What do you mean, "open to suggestion"?' she asked suspiciously.

He still held on to her hands.

'You see things in black and white sometimes. You don't stop to question what you see——' he paused '—or hear, or expect.'

'I don't understand what you mean,' she said in a high, haughty voice. She made a half-hearted attempt to free her hands, but gave in when he grasped them harder.

'In this instance, you saw a ravishing female half undressed, and made assumptions.' He leaned towards her, and she felt his breath on her face. 'And it was only Helen, a relative by marriage. A relative who had a right to be in my house.'

'A beautiful relative.'

'So?' There was a question in his voice.

'I thought you were interested in her, and she looked, dressed like that. . .'

'It's her style. She's one of those rather helpless sorts of women who always need a man, and automatically dress in an ultra-feminine fashion, but a man like me needs more than just a pretty face; I like intelligence and courage to spice my beauty package. Helen can't help being what she is, but I have no interest in her whatsoever as a woman. I told you that I was only helping her sort out her affairs.'

'I'm sorry, I didn't believe you.'

He shrugged. 'I'm not surprised; you couldn't know that Helen had suffered hell over losing her husband, and it was compounded by the fact that she had been given false hope through this wretched homeopathy.'

'Homeopathy?'

'Yes, Duncan, her husband, in the last few weeks of his life was suffering from abdominal cramps and nausea. Nothing seemed to touch it, until he tried some homeopathic medicine, which seemed to relieve him. He appeared to rally for a few days, and Helen thought that he was on the road to recovery. He died quite suddenly, and Helen was devastated, as she had thought that he was getting better. It was the worst thing that could have happened to her.'

'But perhaps not to Duncan, if he had at least a little relief!' Erica suddenly understood Gregory's reluctance to accept alternative medicine; he was concerned for others, as he had once said, for the false hope that it might give. Her heart melted. How like him, always thinking about other people. 'It doesn't always have to be wrong,' she said gently. 'Conventional medicine makes mistakes. He might have had a remission and Helen might have imagined a dramatic improvement.'

Gregory gave her a long, considering look. 'Yes,' he said at last, 'perhaps you're right. But I'd hate to see anyone suffer as Helen suffered; she was so convinced, you see, that he was improving.'

'Poor Helen, and to think that I was jealous of her, and now I feel desperately sorry for her. If I can do anything to help?' She looked at Gregory a little uncertainly, hoping that he understood how she now felt.

'You've got a generous and loving heart, Erica, but I think Helen will manage. In spite of being the frail little woman, she's got reserves of strength that she's not yet aware of.' He smiled gently down at her. 'Now,' he said softly. 'You know all there is to know about Helen; tell me about you and Larry.'

His request took her by surprise. 'There's. . .there's nothing to tell,' she stuttered. 'There never was on my part, though I pretended a little.' She felt herself blushing, remembering how she had tried to make Gregory think that she was interested in Larry.

Gregory nodded and looked pleased with himself. 'I rather thought that was the case. If it hadn't been, you would have witnessed a hell of a reaction from me. I can be jealous too, you know.'

'Can you?' she whispered.

'You'd better believe it. Now we've wasted too much time while you wondered about my feelings for Helen, and let matters fester, like a suppurating wound.'

Gregory's eyes in the dim light were on hers, and her hands were held fast in his.

'I don't know what else to say,' she said weakly, 'except to repeat how sorry I am.'

'What about "I love you"?' he replied.

She caught her breath, and then said slowly, experimentally, savouring the words, 'I love you.'

Gregory waited while she rolled the words round on her tongue. His grip on her hands grew tighter. After a few moments he asked, 'Well?'

'I do love you,' Erica said haltingly. 'I think I always have.'

'Good.' He drew her to him and kissed her, firmly, soundly, without passion. 'Now let's go back to my place and get things sorted out.'

'What things?' she whispered.

'Our future will do for starters,' he said with a wide smile.

He took her hand as they walked across the park with the dogs cavorting about them. She looked back toward Princes, and the lights of the hospital piercing the night behind her. All the wards were brightly lit, including Gregory's cardio-thoracic wards; his world and hers, she thought.

Their future, he'd said! What had he in mind? To Erica, it all seemed faintly unreal. She had expected to do lots of explaining, but had in fact found that Gregory had anticipated her, and wasn't looking for explanations. He had seen only too plainly what had troubled her, and was ready to forgive her. But she wasn't ready to forgive herself.

'I'm so sorry,' she said, 'to have doubted you. I might have known that you would be totally honest.'

Gregory shrugged. 'Why should you know that?' he asked. 'In one way you don't know me very well — although that can be remedied — and I could easily have deceived you.'

'Do you forgive me?'

'There's nothing to forgive. You were unnecessarily jealous of another beautiful woman; what's wrong with that? If anything, I should be flattered to think that I was the reason for your jealousy, that you cared enough for me.' He stopped walking and pulled her into his arms to kiss her again, cupping the back of her head with one large hand as his mouth covered hers.

Erica said breathlessly when he let her go at last, 'But you were so angry with me, so hard.'

'Not because you were jealous, my darling, but because you wouldn't listen to me. You went, as usual, straight into battle, without giving me a chance to defend myself. You're a formidable opponent, my very dear and lovely Erica, and life would be empty without you. These last weeks have been a hollow sham, and I've been like a bear to everyone.'

'Have you?'

'Yes, and that untarnished reputation of mine is likely to vanish unless you agree to marry me.'

It was now quite dark, except for a little starlight. Without warning, he dropped on one knee and took both her hands in his, and said softly, teasing yet serious, 'Please, Miss Erica Lang, will you do me the honour of marrying me?'

Erica looked down at him and giggled. 'Oh, do get up,' she said. 'I'm sure the ground's damp.'

Gregory rose to his feet and towered over her. 'So much for romance,' he said drily. 'I thought it was every woman's ambition to have a man kneel at her feet and propose.'

'One that most of us outgrow when we leave our teens behind. At my age I would much rather go for a proposal of a serious relationship than a pretentious one of marriage.'

He still loomed over her, and now pulled her roughly to him. 'Pretentious?' he growled. 'Are you implying insincere?'

'You didn't really mean marriage, did you?' she whispered.

'What the hell did you think I meant? I'm not in the habit of throwing around phoney proposals.' He looked down at her and relented. 'Of course I meant it, you dear, sweet, silly girl. I love you to distraction, don't you know that? There's an old song which talks about being past love. Well, I thought I was, but I'm not, and I want to marry you and prove it. So will you marry me, Erica?'

For once she didn't want to argue, though there were all sorts of reasons why she might, like not knowing each other for long.

She looked up into his handsome and beloved face. 'Yes, please,' she said. 'As soon as possible.'

They were married at the end of May in the hospital chapel.

Besides their families and friends, many of Princes' staff were present: Matron Clare Dunn, of course, and Luke Steel, the casualty consultant, and Poppy and Nicholas Fordyce from Paediatrics, who had been the last couple to be married in the chapel, earlier in the year.

Lady Violet was there, and Sir Noel Barrington, the chairman of the policy and resources committee. Even Larry Grey, Erica's grateful friend and admirer, had taken time out from his precious pain clinic to be present at the wedding.

As they stood at the chapel door, waiting for photographs to be taken, Gregory looked around at the sea of faces, spread in a semicircle round the church door, and bent down to speak to Erica.

'Aren't we lucky,' he said, 'to have an extended family beyond our blood relations to come and wish us well on our special day?'

'We certainly are,' she said. 'It's wonderful to feel

such a lot of goodwill washing around us. It bodes well for the future.'

'The future, and us, and Princes,' said Gregory, with quiet satisfaction, as the cameras clicked, and he kissed his new wife.

LOVE ON CALL
4 FREE BOOKS AND 2 FREE GIFTS
F R O M   M I L L S   &   B O O N

Capture all the drama and emotion of a hectic medical world when you accept 4 Love on Call romances PLUS a cuddly teddy bear and a mystery gift - absolutely FREE and without obligation. And, if you choose, go on to enjoy 4 exciting Love on Call romances every month for only £1.80 each! Be sure to return the coupon below today to: Mills & Boon Reader Service, FREEPOST, PO Box 236, Croydon, Surrey CR9 9EL.

— — — — — — [**NO STAMP REQUIRED**] — — — — —

YES! Please rush me 4 FREE Love on Call books and 2 FREE gifts! Please also reserve me a Reader Service subscription, which means I can look forward to receiving 4 brand new Love on Call books for only £7.20 every month, postage and packing FREE. If I choose not to subscribe, I shall write to you within 10 days and still keep my FREE books and gifts. I may cancel or suspend my subscription at any time. I am over 18 years. Please write in BLOCK CAPITALS.

Ms/Mrs/Miss/Mr _____ **EP63D**

Address _____

_____

Postcode _____ Signature _____

mps
MAILING
PREFERENCE
SERVICE

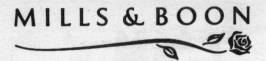

MILLS & BOON

LOVE ON CALL

The books for enjoyment this month are:

SURGEON'S DILEMMA Margaret Barker
A LOVING LEGACY Marion Lennox
FALSE IMPRESSIONS Laura MacDonald
NEVER PAST LOVING Margaret O'Neill

♥　♥　♥　♥　♥

Treats in store!

Watch next month for the following absorbing stories:

PICKING UP THE PIECES Caroline Anderson
IN THE HEAT OF THE SUN Jenny Ashe
LEGACY OF SHADOWS Marion Lennox
LONG HOT SUMMER Margaret O'Neill